The Twenty-Two Year Old Amish Widow

Sarah Amberson

Published by Trellis Publishing, 2021.

This is a work of fiction. Similarities to real people, places, or events are entirely coincidental.

THE TWENTY-TWO YEAR OLD AMISH WIDOW

First edition. July 8, 2021.

Copyright © 2021 Sarah Amberson.

ISBN: 979-8224558292

Written by Sarah Amberson.

THE TWENTY-TWO YEAR OLD AMISH WIDOW

1

SARAH AMBERSON

Emma hurried down the steps of her small home. She was never going to get used to getting up this early. She had always been somewhat of an early riser, but it had been her husband who had tended to the animals before the sun was up.

The thought of her late husband made her heart ache slightly. It had been nearly three years now, and the pain got a little better every day, but it was still there. She still often thought of the things he would do and imagined what he would say when she was alone in the house they had shared.

She wasn't what most people would expect a widow to look like. She was only twenty-two. She had thought that she was married old when she hadn't managed to find a man until she was nineteen. A lot of her friends had found a match when they were eighteen.

She realized now how wrong she had been. She was only twenty-two with her entire life ahead of her, but it would be a lonely life. She made her way to the barn and went about milking the cow, and feeding the two horses deep in thought.

Back when her husband had been alive, they had owned six cows and sold milk in town. They had also made cheese and yoghurt. Now that it was just her, she'd had no choice but to sell all but one of the cows. It was too much work to handle all on her own. Emma still did some baking, selling her little cakes to the small store in town. She made enough to support herself, but she didn't do the livestock for an income anymore.

She patted her favorite horse on the nose, "I'll be back to see you tonight," she said softly.

She loved both of her horses. She had also had to sell several horses because they were too much to handle. But she had kept her two favorite ones because she couldn't bear to part with either of them, and sometimes, she needed them to pull the wagon.

Once she had finished feeding the chickens, all of the chores were taken care of. She went back inside to gather up the products she had prepared the night before to sell. On Fridays when she'd made a lot, she would hook up the horse and buggy and transport her goods that way. But today was Tuesday and there wasn't nearly enough to warrant such a fuss.

Instead, she packed the loaves of bread, soft muffins and jars of strawberry jam into her largest basket. She paused for a moment to admire the beauty of all the packaging sitting together like that, ready to be taken to be sold. She picked up the basket which was heavier than she thought it would be and headed out the door and down the road toward the little store that carried the things she made.

There were lots of people who made the products in the store. There was Mr. Timothy; he had the bee farm and provided the honey. There were different women who made baked goods, clothing, butter, cheese and nearly everything you could think of.

Emma liked that about their little community. The shop that they all contributed to was in a way a mirror of the way that the people in the community took care of each other.

She wondered how it was that Englisher communities were all right with never sharing that sort of bond with their neighbors. Emma felt as if even if she was with without money or food and on the street, her neighbors and her community would care for her.

She hoped that she would never experience how that might feel to be in such a state of need.

"Good morning, Emma. You sure are early today," the young woman tending to the store said with a grin.

Technically, the store belonged to the Yoder family. They were the ones who bought the products from everyone else and then in turn sold them. But Emma knew that in a way the store belonged to everyone who contributed to it, because without products, you couldn't have a store.

"Good morning. Yes, I suppose I overestimated how much time I would need to take care of the animals this morning. How are your parents and your brothers and sisters?"

"They are doing fine. I think that Emily will be taking care of the store later. She said that she wanted to talk to you about something."

"I can wait till she gets here," Emma said, setting her basket on the counter. She was best friends with one of the Yoder's older daughter's, Emily. They were only a year apart, and yet, Emily always had good advice for Emma.

Unlike Emma, Emily had never been married before. The two of them liked to talk and joke and imagine what it would be like for them to find husbands, even though Emily was already twenty-one and Emmy was a widow.

"All right, she shouldn't be long," Emily's sister said.

Emma nodded and took a seat. It seemed that Emily's sister had been telling the truth. A few moments later, Emily walked in. She had a smile on her face as soon as she spotted Emma.

"You're here! I was hoping you would be. I have the best sort of news for you!" Emily gushed before Emma could say a word.

Emma smiled at her friend. She and Emily were so different from each other. They both were the same age and had a lot of things that they both liked, but Emma was quieter and didn't speak her mind as easily as Emily did.

Emily was always bubbly, full of energy and things to talk about. She pulled Emma from her chair. She then proceeded to pull her outside of the store. "You'll never guess what happened."

"What?" Emma asked with a smile. She had a feeling that even if she did try to guess, she wouldn't be able to.

"Michael Grey asked me if I would go riding with him in his buggy next Saturday."

Emma smiled, "That's great news. You have always been hoping that he would."

Emily went on chatting about every detail of her meeting with Michael and how excited she was, but Emma found herself not listening hardly at all. Of course, she was happy for her friend, but it also made her sad, realizing that this part of her life was over now.

Part of her wished that she would have been able to meet her first husband now. Maybe if they hadn't been so young and reckless, he would still be alive. The guilt nibbled at her stomach. She wished she could do so many things differently, but it was too late for that now.

It seemed that while her life was just starting out, at the same time, she had already lived the life most dreamed of. She'd already been married, she'd already built a home of her own.

She'd already lost a husband, grieved for him, suffered for a year in his absence. She had been through so much in a few short years. She often felt as if she were an old person trapped in a young body. But she would never tell Emily that. Her friend couldn't understand the feelings and the memories that bombarded Emma on any given day. And Emma didn't want to make Emily feel badly because of that. Instead, she would try to be there for her friend no matter what and hopefully someday, she wouldn't be alone anymore.

—-*—-

When Emma got back home, the sun was already falling behind the houses, headed for the horizon. Emma had stayed in town the entire day. That hadn't been her intention, but the time had slipped away from her.

She had stayed for several hours talking with Emily and then helping her tend the store just to keep her company. She had then gone to drop off a couple jars of jam with the reverend's wife. She had made them especially for the reverend's wife because they had recently welcomed a new child to their family and Emma hadn't had a chance to bring a gift until now.

She had been invited to stay for lunch with the reverend and his wife and then stayed for nearly two hours afterward. On her way home she had stopped by her brother's home and seen her niece and her brother had gifted her with some broccoli and carrots. She loved seeing her brother's family. It was a little piece of the family she had shared growing up. She missed that, the simplicity of being children and depending on their parents for everything. Sometimes, she thought she would do anything to go back to that innocent stage of her life.

She sighed. She enjoyed visiting in town It was a distraction from the stillness and quiet that surrounded her constantly in her home. She didn't like being alone all the time, feeling badly about her situation. And when she was alone in the house, she could imagine her husband in each room and tried not to think of it. It was just too hard.

But visiting all day made her feel a bit depressed when she finally did arrive home. It made her feel as if the entire day had escaped her, allowing her to get nothing done.

Emma set her brother's gifts inside the house and then hurried out to the barn. She needed to milk the cow and care for the horses before she went inside to eat a little something for dinner and then go to sleep.

She started with the evening chores, milking the cow and checking on the horses. When she was finished with the evening chores, she headed back to the house. The sun had finished it's decent and an inky darkness surrounded her. The moon wasn't hardly out tonight, making the shadows long and darker than normal, sending a chill up Emma's spine.

It wasn't that she was afraid of the dark. It just made her uncomfortable. When Emma made it back to the house, she nearly tripped on the step. A little scream escaped her as she realized there was a person's body thrown across her doorstep.

A moan escaped whoever it was that was resting there. Emma was frozen for a moment, wondering if she should run back to the barn, run to her neighbor's place, or go closer to the figure with her lamp to see who it was and if they were hurt badly.

While her mind and her heart were telling her that one of the first two options would be the best course to take, she stepped toward the figure. She was curious. That was her one flaw. She could rarely turn down her curiosity. She held the lamp down beside the figure and was able to make out the figure of a man.

She gasped, what could have possibly brought this person here to her doorstep? Things like this just didn't happen to her.

He looked to be about her age, but he wasn't someone she knew. In fact, he wasn't Amish at all. He was wearing Englisher clothing and he was clean shaven. His boots looked sort of like military boots that Emma had seen on the men when she had visited the Englishers towns on occasion.

To her surprise, he moved, propping himself up so he was leaning up on one elbow and staring up at her. Emma wasn't sure if she kept still because she wanted to see what he would do or if it was because she was terrified and couldn't do anything else.

A breath escaped her when she saw the man's face. It appeared that any other time he would be quite handsome, but blood streaked his face and his cheek was swollen as if someone had injured him.

"A- are you all right?" Emma asked, a tremor in her voice.

"Who are you?" The man asked, squinting up at her.

"My name is Emma. I live here." Emma knew that she shouldn't answer him or tell him her name. Goodness, she should have never spoken to him in the first place, and yet here she was. "What is your name? What happened to you and what are you doing here?" Emma had a lot more questions for him, but those were the most important to her.

"I'm... I was... I don't know the answer to any of those questions," he finally said, looking confused. The man pulled himself into a sitting position, placing his head in his hands and moaning. "All I remember is that there were people hitting me and I was trying to get away. I don't remember why. I don't know who they were. I don't remember coming here. Where am I?"

"You should go. You can't stay here." Emma felt sympathy for him, but she couldn't keep him here.

"Please, just let me stay the night in your barn. If you'd like, I'll leave first thing in the morning. I don't remember anything, who I am, how I got here... why I'm..." the man touched his hand to his face, and drew it away, examining the blood on his fingers for a moment, "Why I'm hurt. I just need a place to stay for a bit to rest."

"I don't know... if anyone saw you here, they might think the wrong thing." Emma felt uncertain. For some reason, she wanted to help the man. There was something about him that made her want to trust him, despite the fact that she knew nothing about him and despite the fact that someone had obviously been fighting with him.

"All I'm asking is to stay in your barn. You don't have to do anything else. Just pretend you don't know that I am there." The man looked up at her as if she were his last hope in the world.

Emma stared into his eyes. She wanted to tell him to leave, that he couldn't stay and she couldn't possibly help him, but she found different words coming from her mouth instead.

"You can stay, but... try to stay hidden. I don't know what anyone would think if they saw you here." Emma bit her lower lip and watched as the man stood, wobbling a bit as if he were hurt in other places.

"Thank you, thank you so much." The man's eyes were full of gratitude. "I'll be up in the loft. No one will know I am here."

"What should I call you?"

"I- I don't know. I really don't remember my name."

"David, I'll call you David for now." Emma liked the name David. It was a name that reminded her of a childhood friend she had known a long time ago.

"That sounds good. I really can't thank you enough. Don't worry. You won't regret it," David flashed her a weak smile and then started walking toward the barn.

Emma nodded, but she had a feeling that she would. But even so, she couldn't bring herself to tell the man she'd changed her mind, so instead, she turned and walked into the house, ready to find something to prepare for dinner.

—-*—-

David leaned back against the sturdy boards of the barn wall. His head pounded and the cut on his forehead stung. He hadn't been lying to Emma about what he remembered. When he tried to think of his name or how he had gotten to this community, his mind was fuzzy and blank.

He shook his head and drew in a shaky breath. Wherever he had come from, he must have had enemies. If he didn't, how could he have gotten so beat up?

He entered the barn and looked around. There were four stalls toward the front of the barn. Three of them had animals in them. The cow and horses looked at him with curious eyes.

He found the ladder at the back of the barn and slowly climbed it. Twice he had to stop as his vision blurred and he was afraid he might lose consciousness again. At the top of the ladder he looked around briefly and they stumbled to the back of the loft where there was a cleared area behind several stacked haybales. He sat down between two bales and leaned back on a pile of loose hay. He pulled some of the soft fresh hay closer around him to stay warm.

David wondered why Emma lived here alone. She looked so young and he hadn't seen anything to indicate that a man lived here with her.

He sighed, wondering what he was going to do the next day. He didn't even know what direction to go to get to where he had come from.

A noise made him sit up a little straighter. Someone was coming to the barn. He heard the sound of someone climbing the ladder. The soft glow of a lamp bobbed up and down until it stopped right above him. He squinted up to see Emma there. She was holding a tray in one hand and a bucket in the other.

"Emma, I wasn't expecting to see you here. Is something wrong?" David wondered if she had come to tell him that she had changed her mind and wanted him gone as soon as he could stand. He certainly hoped that wasn't the case because he wasn't sure how well he could walk.

"I brought you some dinner," Emma said kindly. "And I need to take care of your wounds."

"Are you sure? I don't want to be an inconvenience." David wasn't sure what experience from the past had made him feel this way, but something was telling him that he didn't want to impose on Emma or make things difficult for her.

"It's no trouble," she said. She put the bucket and a bundle on a haybale. Emma knelt down on her knees in front of him. She extended the tray which was full of food toward him. There was a sandwich that appeared to be made from chicken and cheddar cheese with lettuce and tomatoes. There were two chocolate pastries and a big glass of what appeared to be lemonade.

David reached out and took a bite of the sandwich, his stomach growled in both satisfaction and need. He was starving, famished. Who knew how long it had been since he'd eaten something?

"I'm going to wipe off the blood," Emma already had a cloth in her hand and was reaching for his forehead.

He hesitated a moment, but then kept still and allowed her to tend to his wounds. The washcloth was warm against his skin. He winced as she gently wiped away the blood and whatever else was on his face.

She then applied a cream to his cuts which stung at first, but then left them feeling better, tingling with warmth.

"Why are you helping me?" David asked, readjusting himself and taking another bite of the food she had brought him.

He hadn't expected this from her. He had figured that the next morning he would have to be on his way to figure out this mystery on his own.

He didn't mind her helping him. In fact, he rather liked it. It made him feel a bit safer and better about his predicament. But she had seemed so uncertain about helping him before.

"I- it's been a while since I have actually done something because I wanted to. And helping you, I feel like it is something that I want to do, regardless of what others might think."

"If there are some things that need some repair done, I could help around the place if you'd allow me to. Maybe by tomorrow I will feel a little stronger."

He shook his head ever so slightly. He had adapted to the name David with little difficulty, even though he was sure that his real name must be something different.

"Actually, that's not a bad idea. In exchange for a place to stay and food, I wouldn't mind some extra help while you figure things out." Emma smiled and David couldn't help but think that it lit up her face and made her eyes glow.

It was a beautiful sight to see. He wondered why she didn't smile more often, though maybe that was just because he hadn't known her long.

"I should go, but I hope you sleep well, David. Oh, I brought you a blanket and pillow," she added as she nodded to the folded bedding on the haybale next to him. Emma stood and gathered the empty dishes that had held the food he had just finished eating and the things she had used to tend to him.

He watched her go until she'd disappeared down the ladder, leaving the place feeling just a little colder in her absence.

He pulled the blanket she'd brought him up around his shoulders and leaned back against the straw on the pillow. He didn't know where he was used to sleeping, but this was about as comfortable as things got.

—-*—-

Emma stared out the kitchen window. It had been nearly a week since David had shown up on her doorstep. He had been true to his word and done a huge amount of work on her little ranch that she hadn't even known needed to be done.

Today, he was fixing the front pasture by the barn. She watched him as he set a beam across between the two pillars of the fence and went about securing it. There was something about him that attracted her.

He was always so calm and collected and very kind and polite. He was certainly not what she expected of an outsider man. Every day he was up early in the morning, taking care of one task after another, not needing to be asked to do things and he didn't ask her for any favors or appear to expect any.

Emma shook her head. She didn't know what she was going to do with him. She knew that the rest of town was going to realize he was there eventually. Even though he had been sleeping in the barn and hadn't gone into town, it would only be a matter of time till someone saw him and then talked to someone else. She hadn't really gone into town since he'd come, so for all she knew the entire community could be talking about her already.

She looked over at the rows of baked goods that sat on her counter. It was the weekend and she needed to deliver these to the store. The bread would only be fresh for a day.

She sighed, then turned her gaze back to David. She wondered how long he would stick around. It was going to be sad when he left.

She took a plate of food she had prepared for him only shortly before and a large glass of water out to the front porch.

"David, your lunch is ready," she called out to him.

He looked up at her, waved and then smiled. She felt a flutter in her heart. Something she hadn't felt toward anyone since her husband died. She wondered how she could possibly have that sort of reaction toward David. She hardly knew him. Goodness, he didn't even know himself. How could she be thinking of such things?

She pushed the thoughts back and set the food on the porch table and then headed back inside to finish getting her bread and jam ready for the store. David had already hooked the horses to the buggy a little before and they were waiting impatiently for her when she got outside.

"Where did you learn to hook horses to a buggy? It's not a skill everyone has," Emma asked with a grin as she stepped out on to the porch with her first box of goods.

"I am not sure. Just like everything else about me I know how to do some things but I can't remember how I learned them." David's eyebrows knit together in a worried look. "You know, I kind of wish that my old life would just stay in the past and I could stay here forever and forget about it."

"Me too," Emma found herself saying before she could think about her words. She giggled nervously, "I should be going," she added softly.

"I'll be here when you get back." David gave her a grin. "Thank you for lunch. It was really good."

Emma hurried to finish loading the buggy and then quickly headed to town. She wasn't sure how to feel about the fact that she felt comforted to know that David would be there when she got back.

—-*—-

The smell of smoke tickled David's nose. He was standing in the middle of a street, the rocks cutting into his bare feet.

He turned to see a building was burning not too far away. The sign that read, "Hotel," had fallen on one side of its hinges and only a small bit of the original sign was hanging down, a remnant of the beauty the hotel had been.

David looked down to see the limp body of a child in his arms. The boy was still breathing. He could feel it against his chest. A man came running from the fire, a woman in his arms. He set her down and started to push on her chest, in his efforts to revive her. David could tell that it was too late for the woman. He knew who she was. She was the mother of the child he held in his arms.

He looked down at the little boy who had lost his mother but still didn't know it. The man who had carried the woman out rushed toward him.

"Why didn't you save her? You could have saved her too!" he screamed.

David knew that the man was just upset, but still, his words stung.

He held out the child to the man who took the boy, tears streaming down his face. "Why didn't you save her too?" the man asked a second time.

"I'm sorry. I couldn't carry both of them. She told me to take the boy. She told me to take him instead of her. She wanted him to live." David shook his head back and forth. He reached up and touched his forehead. His hand came away with blood. A beam from the hotel had fallen on him before he was able to escape the place.

No one had expected the place to light on fire. Not even him. Why couldn't he have known? Why couldn't he have woken up sooner? He could have saved them both. Andrew, that was his real name. He remembered now, he remembered everything.

David woke with a start. His face was wet with tears and he was trembling and breathing hard. He sat up in his bed of hay and looked around at the familiar loft. The moon was shining in through the singular window casting its silver light across the haybales stacked there.

Even though he remembered that his name was Andrew, he didn't want to go back to being Andrew. Suddenly small details of his life came rushing back. How he used to work at a bank, and had been traveling when he had chosen to stay at a hotel.

He remembered now how the hotel had started on fire and he'd been faced with the worst choice of his life, to save the mother or her child, and he had been blamed for that choice by the man who was surely the woman's husband.

The memories bombarded him. He had been a loner, with no family and even fewer friends. He had had nothing to look forward to and that night at the hotel, things had even seemed more dismal.

In the past three weeks working for Emma, he had felt happy and fulfilled, seeing her face light up with every new project he did for her.

He had become used to this simple life, of tending to animals and the buildings around the tiny farm that Emma called her home. He didn't want these memories that had come back so quickly out of nowhere. He would have been happier if his old life had stayed buried forever.

That night at the hotel, when the beam had fallen on his head, he must have injured himself somehow and lost his memory after leaving the fire. He shook his head. He was confused though. He remembered someone beating him. Had that happened after? Maybe he had been robbed when he had wandered off.

He didn't feel like he could go back to sleep so he climbed down the ladder and headed outside. Maybe he would go for a walk.

He was surprised to see that Emma was still up. Maybe he hadn't actually been asleep for that long.

Emma was sitting on the porch, and waved to him as he walked uncertainly out of the barn. She looked happy to see him and it broke his heart. He knew he needed to tell her everything about his old life, but David wasn't ready to give up his new life. He was afraid maybe she wouldn't want to be his friend anymore if she knew how he had failed but it wasn't fair to keep his past from her either.

His palms were sweaty and his mouth felt suddenly dry. How could he feel so nervous about this? He had never felt this nervous when thinking of speaking with Emma before.

He was going to tell her what he really wanted, to stay here as David, to continue to help her, even though he was no longer the David she knew. He wondered what she would think of him once she knew who he really was.

He ran a hand through his tousled hair and approached the porch cautiously. "Is it ok if I come talk to you?" he asked nervously.

"What's wrong? You look... worried." Emmy straightened in her chair, a look of concern on her face.

"I remember who I am now. I was asleep and started dreaming and when I woke up I remembered."

"Oh," Emma's face fell, and she looked as disappointed as he felt. "What did you remember?"

"I remember who I was, and what happened the night I came here or at least most of it. Can we talk?" David sat down across from her.

"Of course. I want to know who you really are, David," Emma said softly.

He closed his eyes and then opened them, starting to tell her his story, hoping they would still be friends after he was done.

—-*—-

When David stopped talking, Emma felt a huge wave of relief. She had been so worried he would tell her something terrible. That he had been a criminal or he had hurt someone. But to know that the only thing that was in his past was sadness and normal issues that every person faced in their life made her feel hopeful.

"Are you angry?" David was looking at her with concern.

"Angry? Why would I be angry?" Emma was feeling a lot of emotions, but anger was not one of them.

"Because, I know that before I remembered who I was, I was a blank slate in a way, a new person who was just the person you got to know. Now you know that I am not an Amish man. You know that my life has been very different to the life I have lived here. I grew up on a farm but I haven't ever been Amish."

"That is not a bad thing. Every person lives differently. I was so worried that your past would have been something terrible that... well, in all honesty, I couldn't be happier about what your memories are. It is terrible what happened the night of the fire, but you helped how you could. You shouldn't blame yourself for not being able to save both of them. I'm sure the man was just grieving because he lost his wife but I'm sure he was thankful that you saved his son."

David smiled sadly. "I want to ask you one more thing."

"What is it?" Emma's heart filled with hope. There was one thing that she hoped that David would ask, but it was probably too much to ask for. He was used to an Englisher life, he was used to the comforts outside of the Amish community, and yet she held her breath, waiting for him to keep talking.

"Emma, in the past few weeks while I have worked here, I have found a deep appreciation for the simple life that you lead. I have also... well, I have gotten used to seeing you, to working with you every single day. I know that I am a different person than the one you found that night but..." David paused and Emma's heart beat hard in her chest "Emma if you would give me a chance, I would love to stay here and continue working for you, get to know you as Andrew, the real me."

Emma paused, trying to gather all of her thoughts before speaking. This felt so unreal, like a dream. "Do you really mean it?"

"Of course, I mean it. I wouldn't say it otherwise."

Emma's eyes filled with tears. "You know, ever since my husband died, I have felt loneliness, creeping up on me, filling my heart a little more every single day. And then you showed up and you made me laugh and made me feel as if I wasn't so alone anymore. I know this sounds silly, but I feel like I already know you, the real you, even though you didn't have your memories before."

David's face seemed to slowly light up. "So, you would like me to stay?"

"I'd like that very much," she answered.

"What about the fact that I am not Amish? I like this lifestyle, so much. But I would need to think about everything that it entails. I would have to fully understand what I was putting myself into before fully committing."

"It's all right." Emma bit her lower lip. "Whatever you decide, we will talk about it when you know what you want. I'm sure the elders would need to talk to you so that you could truly understand our way of life. If you were to join the Amish you would need to join the church and you would need to understand what that commitment would mean."

"Thank you, I never thought... I never thought that you might share the same feelings or desires to get to know me like I did you. I have to admit I was preparing for the worst when I remembered and came to talk with you."

Emma giggled with relief. "I was just thinking the same. I couldn't be happier, David... I mean, Andrew. I think that maybe, maybe we met each other for a reason."

"I think you are right." David said softly. "I think you are right."

Emma smiled and took a deep breath. She didn't know exactly what would happen in the upcoming months. But she did know that in the past several weeks, she had come to care for David in a special way. She also knew that even though David had remembered that his real name was Andrew, essentially, he was the same person she had come to care for.

She had a feeling that this was the beginning of a beautiful adventure, and she also had a feeling that maybe, she would no longer be alone for the rest of her life, and that was one of the most encouraging things that had ever happened to her.

AMISH WISHES

JESSICA PENN

1.

Tracing her finger over the cold, gray tombstone, Joanna inhaled deeply and choked back a sob. Kneeling in the pasture of their family's cemetery, she placed a bouquet of daffodils in front of the stone. It all felt like a dream to her. She didn't think she would ever lose her mother. She was her best friend and now that she was gone Joanna felt lost. She spoke softly to the stone just as she would as if her mother were standing beside her. "Hello, Mother. I miss you more each day. I really wish you could have stayed. It's lonely here without you. Everyone is trying to be strong. They want to continue life as it was before, but without you being here, it's impossible. I know you're in a better place and you're not in pain from the illness ravaging your earthly body, but it's still hard. I just don't know what to do now. I have assumed all of your household duties, just as you would have wished, but I find myself feeling increasingly empty. None of this feels right." Before she could finish her conversation, she heard the distinctive sound of horses clopping in the distance. She knew her brothers would be coming to take her back to their small home in the center of their community. They would have finished their errands in town, and she would be needed soon to start preparing supper. Dusk would be upon them soon, and after evening services, a good meal, a nice fire, and sleep would be arriving soon.

Joanna stood up slowly and ran her fingers along the cold stone one more time, giving a weak smile of recognition to her brother, Eli, who trotted up on his prized horse, Petunia. Petunia was a gentle creature and was easily broken. Eli was good to the creature and she respected him as well, she wouldn't ever buck him off, even when they were traveling through thunderstorms or if she ran up on a snake in the tall weeds. They trusted one another. Joanna could say the same about her brother, even though she was the older sibling, they trusted one another and vowed to always protect one another through all of life's trials. Eli looked down from Petunia and frowned. He hated to see his sister suffer so, but as a young man, he knew that for the good of the community he couldn't let his own sorrows show. He had to be strong for his sister now and show nothing but unconditional support. Now was the time for them to come together as a family and keep each other close. That's what his mother would have wanted. "It's good to see you, sister. Are you ready to return to the house?"

Joanna looked up at Eli's eyes and knew that behind the deep brown spheres, there was a touch of sadness that lingered there. He was trying so hard to put on a brave front, but she knew the truth, he wouldn't be the same after their mother's passing either. "Yes. I'm ready to return, Eli. Can I ride with you?"

"Of course. I think Petunia has it in her to walk us both back home along the path." The horse merely whinnied and they both laughed at her response. As they trotted along the path, Joanna's voice turned solemn once again as she asked, "How's father today?"

"He didn't say much at all, he merely got up and went into his study, where he read some scriptures and made some notes for service, then he walked out into the garden and surveyed the crops. It was like a typical day for him it seems."

"I wish he would express himself more."

"Ah, you know how he is Joanna, that's how he always was, stoic and stone-faced."

"Yeah. Maybe one day we'll figure him out."

"Ha! You have jokes, my sister. I seriously have my doubts about that."

They rode back up to the house in relative silence only listening to the sounds of the birds chirping and the echo of Petunia's hooves against the ground. Reaching the house, the pair dismounted and Eli walked Petunia to the barn, taking care to make sure she had plenty of fresh hay and water. Joanna went straight into the house and immediately made her way to the kitchen. In her mind's eye, she could still see her mother standing by the stove, stirring a pot or leaning over to get a knife from the bottom drawer. It was up to her now to make sure the family was fed. She sighed heavily and reached up above the family's ice box to take down a larger pot which hung above it. It was cast iron and the same one that had been used in the family for generations to make hearty stews and soups. That night Joanna decided she would make the family a hearty beef stew. They had some extra meat frozen already in the icebox and she had plenty of canned vegetables from the summer and fall's gardening. She poured some water that had already been carried inside into the large cast iron pot and lit the fire beneath their wood and coal stove. When it came to a full boil she added the meat and vegetables. Her mother had always tried to make her stews last for a few days and made it a point to ensure it was filling as well. Joanna added some corn starch to thicken the broth and proceeded to flavor it with spices. When her father walked into the kitchen, he hung his head, but then looked up and met Joanna's eyes, giving her a slight nod of approval. When the preparations were finished Joanna carried the pot along with some freshly baked bread out to the dining room. The family took their assigned places around the square table. In their mourning period, it was customary to set an extra place at the table for the lost as well, so her mother's chair while empty next to her father, had a place setting and was served some stew as well. It would be her father's task to consume it.

2.

After all was seated, her father spoke. "Good evening my son and daughter. Let us all rejoice and give thanks for what the day hath brought forth. Now is the time we must graciously give thanks for the abundance the Lord hath provided us with and draw close together as a family in our hour of need. I was reading the scriptures this morning and they brought me much comfort. Despite our loss, I trust each of my children to go on living and continue to be upstanding and show true grace. Now let us break bread and honor the fallen."

They all opened their eyes and lifted their heads watching their father who broke the first bit of bread. He then passed the plate to the others who took their portions and set the tray back in the center of the table. Their meal was eaten in silence and no one dared to speak until their simple supper was finished. Their father then looked at each of them and smiled. Tufts of white hair showed his age and he had a natural ruddiness to his skin tone that made him look jovial. He also had lines etched along his forehead left by the many years of being contemplative. One would look at him and assume he was a stern man all of the time, but he had crows feet and smile lines along his eyelids that told another story. While their father was stern and quiet, Joanna could remember a time when they were children he would play their games with them and tell stories which made all of them laugh joyously. He was a man dedicated to worship, but he also was a man who prided himself on the family he had created.

Rising from the table Joanna began to gather the dishes and place them in the kitchen sink, as she crossed into the other room she heard her father say, "Joanna, I'm very pleased with all the progress you have made in the kitchen with meal preparations. Your mother, rest her soul, would be very proud of you." Tears formed in Joanna's eyes and she bit her bottom lip to choke back a sob. Her mother, Annabelle, had been gone now for over a month, but the loss still stung. Her entire family was stuck living with the reminders of her being. Joanna still hadn't had the heart to clean out her closet or her sewing room. The elders had planned a town gathering at the end of the month, however, so she thought she would take them then and donate them. After all, she was a practical woman, just like her mother before her, and knew that there was no sense in good pieces of clothing going to waste when someone less fortunate could be using them. She responded to her father when returning to the table for a second trip for the remainder of the dishes. "Thank you father, I appreciate it. I discover more techniques every day. I feel personal growth is important, don't you?"

"Why, of course it is, Joanna. I've watched you and Eli grow through the years and I'm proud of both of you. I personally feel comforted by the fact that no matter how many times I go to complete a task and fail, I always have another opportunity to give it another try. That's the beauty in salvation and forgiveness. As humans, we all fall short of perfection, but there's always the chance to redeem yourself through prayer and multiple attempts."

Eli cleared his throat and spoke for the first time since they arrived home. "I'm glad for that. I know that there have been many times I felt lost or like I was on the wrong path, but I would pray about it and then something would happen or suddenly change in my life." Joanna listened to the pair talk from the kitchen while washing up the supper dishes and smiled. She loved her father and brother dearly but felt lost. She had no one to talk about her daily affairs with now that her mother had passed. She couldn't tell her father about the gossip she overheard while getting notions for sewing. She couldn't talk to her brother about a certain feeling she had in the pit of her stomach when she watched the baker's son splitting wood while hanging their linens out to dry.

She listened as their conversation continued. Her father spoke in a good-natured tone and there was nothing condescending in his voice as he elaborated on the subject matter with his son. "Eli, do you remember that time you came home crying when you were thirteen or fourteen? It was late in the evening and mid-summer. You had just returned from Mrs. Hollister's barn dance, she was having to raise money for the local town orphanage. You came to me and had tears in your eyes and your lips were swollen and shaking. I'll never forget how dejected you looked."

"Yes, father. I remember that well. I had gone to the dance and got quite upset when I saw Pamela Davison dancing with my friend, James."

"Do you remember what I told you?"

"No, I can't say I can recall, though it must have worked, I haven't harbored feelings for Pamela since that night."

"What I told you then son, was that sometimes we think we know what's best for ourselves, but in the end, it's not us who is ultimately in control of that. Our actions may influence our day to day activities, but it is only through faith we can fulfill our ultimate destiny. Our almighty father wants us to be happy, but sometimes we have to learn a lesson the hard way so we don't pursue other things. Your courtship with Pamela, for example, is one of those things. Do you know what she's doing now?"

"No, father. I haven't a clue."

"She decided to go live among the outsiders. Her life has not been beneficial from it, given my understanding. The last news we received in a letter that she decided to pursue her career as a professional dancer. It turns out that career path led her to work in a nightclub for exotic dancing and she's developed a drug addiction. It's in my best estimation that she will more than likely spend a great deal of her life in prison for drug related crimes or prostitution. So, son, as you can see sometimes our Father doesn't answer our prayers for a reason."

"What if I could have changed her? If she stayed with me, then maybe she would have just lived her life pursuing the path of righteousness."

"Well, I know how susceptible young men are to the wiles of women and their charms. I think that given the choice, you would have left and gone with her and been corrupted by the outside world as well. Outside of our community, there is a temptation to pursue wrongdoing on every corner. No matter what your vice, there is some way to purchase it or attain it there. Never forget that on your travels, Eli."

"I won't Father."

3.

Joanna listened to their conversation while she continued to tidy up the dinner dishes. She knew that her mother would have loved that their father was attempting to socialize with his children, but she also knew that her mother would have played devil advocate in the conversation. She wasn't like most of the other women in the town. She was outspoken and often had heated debates on matters of faith or business with her father, yet they worked to balance each other out very well. Joanna was convinced that when God made her mother, his creation was done purely to spite her father and keep him in line.

She cleaned up the sink and then decided she would go ahead and get the percolator ready for the morning's coffee. She knew that would be the first thing their father would ask for when he woke up in the morning. He often preferred the strong brew first thing, then would go out to complete his chores, foregoing breakfast until their animals had been fed. He always said that if one took care of the animals, they would, in turn, take care of you. He lived by this strict routine day in and day out, with little variation in routine, save for the day he celebrated his wedding anniversary with his wife. On that day, both their father and mother would take a rare trip to town, where they would return with not only small gifts for the children but some goods, that were less costly to purchase such as new blades for the farming equipment. Joanna always dreamed of the outside world as being some type of magical realm where everyone had access to things like running water and life was easy, but as she grew older she realized the outsiders weren't much different than those in her own community. She wasn't allowed to do much traveling into town, but when she did she just noticed that the outsiders seemed to base their own value on their material belongings. This concept just simply didn't exist in her community, everything was shared.

Joanna saw that it was dark now outside and with her chores attended to, she didn't see the point in staying with the menfolk talking around the dinner table. Drying her hands on a dish towel, she decided to go ahead and excuse herself. Walking around the side of the table she approached her father and placed her hand on the side of his chair then leaned over kissing him on the forehead. "I'm going to go ahead and turn in for the evening, father. The nightly chores are all completed."

"Ah, yes, very good little one. My precious daughter. You have sweet dreams and remember that your father and brother are here if you have night terrors."

"Oh, papa. I love you. I haven't had a night terror, though, since I was seven years old."

"Still.. think good thoughts."

"I will. Goodnight. Goodnight Eli."

"Goodnight, sister, remember I love you even in your slumber."

"I will."

Joanna walked to her bedroom and lit the small candle that was on her nightstand, it provided enough light to read by, which is the only thing she enjoyed doing in the evenings to relax. Taking off her bonnet, she sat on the edge of the bed and began undoing the long braids she had in her hair. She preferred to keep it pulled up and away from her face during the course of the day since she was often doing chores. The tresses undid themselves easily and she fluffed hands through it, taking her hairbrush and running it through her long brown locks. After she put on her nightgown and hung her daytime dress back up in her standing closet, she picked up her Bible, seeing the notes she had made in the margins. She had been studying a chapter in Revelations that her father recommended. He felt that it would benefit the family to examine the reasons for death together, so they could make some sense of their mother's unexpected passing. She sighed and remembering her place decided she would finish reading and analyzing the chapter when she arose the following morning. Instead, she picked up the paperback she had borrowed from the town's library. It had a handsome cowboy on the front of it and he appeared in front of a herd of galloping horses. He was holding a blonde woman in his arms and she was swooning. Joanna smiled as the opened the book to the place she left off. It wasn't customary for women in her community to read much at all, but she enjoyed the thoughts of romance and found nothing wrong with dreaming about a handsome cowboy of her own. She finished the chapter and blew out her candle, reclining on her twin bed and closing her eyes sleeping almost immediately.

4.

As the dawn peeked through the clouds, Joanna was awakened by Eli, barging into her bedroom unannounced. He let the door bang on the hinges and had a panicked look on his face, as Joanna pulled the covers up over herself asked, "Why, Eli?! Whatever is the matter?! Is it Father?! Is he okay?!"

"Yes. Oh, Joanna, I'm worried. It's Petunia. She's fallen ill I'm afraid. Can you come out to the barn?"

Breathing out a sigh of relief, Joanna nodded and said, "Of course dear brother. Don't be fearful. The Lord will protect Petunia. Give me a few moments to get decent and I will be out there." Joanna calmly got up from her bed and walked to her closet, taking a few moments to pull her hair back and put on her bonnet then putting on her daytime dress. She pulled the laces tight on her boots and hurried out to the barn where she could see Eli standing by Petunia's stall pacing anxiously. "Thank you for coming out sister. I can't figure out what's wrong with her. She won't respond to my coaxing and she's just lethargic. I've never seen her in this state."

"Calm yourself, Eli. Your panicked state is doing her no good either. Animals can sense your fear." Joanna walked up to the mare who was laying down and looked into Petunia's deep brown eyes. She then placed her hand gently on the creature's forehead. She then stroked the animal's head and back, making soothing sounds, just as her mother would do them when they were sick youngsters. "Yes. You're right to have come to fetch me. She's definitely fallen ill. Let's just hope its a bug. Father has a trip planned to go into town to gather some new ax blades for the fall cutting. I'll go with him and stop by the library and see if I can find a cure in some of the veterinary medicine books they have shelved. Don't worry, brother. We will do what we can for her. Just be fervent in your prayers and there will be a way delivered."

Joanna walked back into the home and began preparing her father's morning coffee. Daylight had just broke and she knew he would be happy to get the day started like normal. When he walked in the kitchen he smiled seeing her standing at the stove as her mother would have, fixing his coffee and preparing breakfast for her brother. Eli always had a voracious appetite She set the steaming mug in front of him and said, "Good morning, Father. I must confess it's already been eventful."

"Oh, really how so?"

"It seems Petunia has fallen ill. I was hoping it would be okay if I went with you while you were in town today to look up some medicine for her at the library."

"I certainly hate to hear that Petunia has taken a turn for the worse. She has been good to our little family. I think that's a wonderful idea darling. God can work miracle cures, but only if we're willing to do a bit of the work as well. After the morning feeding, we will go into town. Be prepared. While I'm purchasing the new blades for the fall wood harvest, you can look into a cure for our Petunia. I bet your brother is worried sick."

"Oh, he is Father. You know he's always been close to the mare."

"We shall do what we can. Thank you for the finely brewed cup of coffee. Now I must get to work, the daylight is already streaming upon us and the chickens will be happy to receive their breakfast."

"Thank you, Father."

Joanna finished making the biscuits and gravy for breakfast then poured them all glasses of freshly squeezed orange juice from the assortment of oranges that they had traded for in town earlier in the summer. She knew their shelf life would be expiring soon and didn't want anything to go to waste. Waste not, want not, her mother always said. She also knew that they all need to keep their strength up because as soon as they got back from town the entire community would gather and chop wood for their collective heat in the winter. After completing her chores and cleaning up the cooking utensils she set the meal on the dining room table and gathered her bag for their trip into town. She made certain she had her city library card and decided to take her paperback with her and exchange it for another as it was nearing completion anyway. Looking around the empty room she sighed. She was worried about her brother, but also she felt a doubt creeping into her soul and a generalized discomfort, wondering if this is how the remainder of her days would be spent, taking care of her father and brother , never knowing the love of a man or having her own family to raise.

Her father and brother came back into the house after feeding the animals and sat down at the table, nodding in appreciation at having their meal already set before them. Eli spoke then, asking to say the morning prayers and included a blessing for his favorite mare as well. They ate the rest of their meal in silence and Joanna immediately went to the sink and began cleaning up the dishes, so she wouldn't have to do both the breakfast and dinner dishes before bed. She also was anticipating having a busy day tending to Petunia upon their return. Her father came and got her when the horses were hitched up to the wagon and her brother helped her climb in beside him. Her father gave his horses a quick pat on the head and they departed on their journey into town.

5.

Arriving in the nearest town, Joanna took in her surroundings as her father hitched up the wagon to the hitching post by the hardware store. She got out of the buggy, amidst the stares of the townspeople. She imagined she looked quite strange to then in her pale blue day dress, with her hair pinned up in a bonnet, while her father was dressed head to toe in all black, complete with his wide-rimmed black hat. His long brown beard wasn't shaved, merely groomed and it did betray his age, as spots of gray could be seen in it when the sun hit it just right. He spoke briefly to his daughter before going inside the store. "Remember daughter, be polite to the townspeople, but do not engage in lengthy conversation unless it pertains to spreading the Gospel. I will be here when you are ready to leave but try to find the information you seek quickly. I suspect this lost time will hurt our productivity later and we won't be able to get as much done as we should. Be careful, Joanna."

Joanna nodded and hugged her father before crossing the street and rounding the block heading to the library. She cast her eyes downward mostly only looking up periodically to dodge obstacles. She opened the doors to the city library and the pleasant librarian smiled and waved at her when she entered. She smiled back and returned the greeting. She liked the librarian, who never questioned her when she came in even as a little girl clutching her mother's skirts. The older clerk would give her lollipops when her mother checked out her religious books and romance novels. Now Joanna was grown and even though she didn't get a lollipop, she still felt those warm feelings when she was in the library. She walked up to the desk and quietly dropped her book on the counter. "I need to return this, and I will be getting another one if I can find the other information I need in time."

"Sure thing, Joanna. Have you been doing okay, since your mother's passing?"

"Oh, yes we have been doing alright, thank you. I'm sorry I was in such a bad state when you saw me last. I am adjusting to this new normal."

"Well, that's good. If you need anything, you let me know as always."

"I will. I will see you when I return."

Joanna then walked off, smiling once more at the clerk. She rounded the corner to the reference desk where there was no clerk, but there was a younger looking man in grease-stained coveralls standing by the finance books, looking bewildered. Joanna watched him pull out a book from the shelf as the rest came tumbling down. She couldn't stifle a small giggle as he fumbled trying to catch them all. He turned around hearing her laughter and she was met with a sheepish smile and the most striking blue eyes she'd ever seen. He took her by surprise as she felt her heart beat faster within her chest and suddenly heat rose to her face as she blushed deeply. Before she could say a word he smiled broadly at her and said, "They don't make these shelves the way they used to do they?"

Joanna giggled once again and said, "No. They certainly don't."

"I don't really know much about this place. I needed a book on taxes, I own my own mechanic shop and I'm doing my own this year to save money for the business. Maybe I should have just paid someone."

"Well, what are you looking for? Maybe I can help."

"A book to tell me how to do it."

Joanna paused for a moment surveying the shelves then reached down to the bottom one, accidently brushing the man's hand as she picked up a hefty volume and placed it in his arms. "Here you go. This will guide you through the process."

"Oh wow. Thank you. I appreciate that ma'am. It's nice to meet you, my name's David."

"I'm Joanna. I'm not from around here, as you can tell."

David took a step toward her, closing the distance, and Joanna felt a certain electricity pass through them. She let the heat rise to her cheeks again and once more looked into his blue eyes. He was in good shape and looked strong from his work. He had blonde hair and was clean shaven. He didn't look like any of the men from their community, but he did seem to possess the same kindness behind his eyes and good spirit. He responded by saying, "I wish you were from around here. I'd hire you to do my taxes."

She chuckled at his joke, then suddenly remembered her purpose. "I really hate to cut on conversation short, David, but I have to get some information then return to my community, my brother's horse is sick and needs medical attention I know nothing of."

"Oh, I'm sorry to hear that. Maybe I can help. I grew up on a ranch."

She couldn't believe her ears. She had wanted a cowboy all of her own. Could it be that her prayers had been answered? He seemed so genuine and caring. She explained the problem with Petunia and David gave her the information she needed to attend to the mare. He reassured her it was nothing major that some tender loving care couldn't fix. He then went on to say that his specialty in life was fixing broken things. Joanna considered the gravity of his statement before turning to leave and decided to do something she would need to ask forgiveness for later.

"You have been so helpful David, could I have your address?"

"Only if I can have yours too."

The pair exchanged addresses and Joanna exited the library, turning around to see David staring at her making her exit. She didn't know what had come over her, but she knew in her heart this man was her destiny.

6.

She exited the library to find her father standing red-faced by the door, checking his pocket watch. She hadn't realized how much time had passed talking with David, she only knew that it felt like they had known each other a lifetime. Feeling the need to apologize she spoke to her father, when they crossed to the buggy, "I'm sorry, father. It took me longer to get the information I needed than what I thought."

He didn't say anything, but merely nodded and coaxed the horses out of the lot and towards the path back to their community. Her father finally spoke when they were close to the halfway point between town and their village. "You know why we caution each other when talking with townspeople? It's not because our religion has restrictions on being social and making friends. In fact, we are encouraged to witness to everyone we possibly can. It's because not all people are righteous, Joanna. Not everyone will have your best interest at heart, and the original evil does find its way into the hearts of men. Some of the people you encounter in the outside world, well let's say the majority of them, only are interested in preying on the weak. It's their life's goal, not helping others or doing good."

Joanna turned her eyes downward again as her father patted her on the leg continuing, "Remember, no matter what happens, Joanna, your family will always support you within the community. We, however, could not help you should you decide to live among the outsiders. You would be shunned and on your own, you know it's our way, there's no changing that." Joanna nodded in acknowledgment, silently rubbing the piece of paper in her pocket which had David's address on it. She knew in her heart, that she needed to see the mysterious cowboy mechanic once again, but didn't like the idea of her father's disapproval. He would never allow such a thing, she felt conflicted and sick at heart the entire way home.

Arriving back at the community they were greeted by Eli, whose worried look had only grown more exasperated during their time away. "Greetings, Father. Greetings, Sister. Did you acquire the knowledge you sought?"

"I did brother. Let's go to the barn and see what we can do."

Together they walked to the barn and checked on Petunia. Joanna took care to follow David's precise instructions and administered a careful mixture of salt brine and water to the mare who greedily lapped it up. It had seemed that she had just gotten a bit dehydrated during their previous days' activities and was feeling under the weather. They monitored her condition throughout the day and it did improve as she eventually got up and started wandering back and forth in her stall, anxious for a trot. In addition to that the new blade purchase, expedited the wood cutting process and the community made short work of the wood pile, stockpiling enough wood to last the entire winter in half the time it normally would. They decided as a community to celebrate their recent accomplishment and give thanks to the Lord, with a feast to be held that upcoming Saturday night.

Joanna spent the night quietly in her room after supper and allowed herself to think of David. She knew beyond a shadow of a doubt that she needed him in her life. She believed, despite her father's warnings that there were good and decency in his soul. No one without a good heart, would have freely given her that information she needed to help her animal. Most of the outsiders would have offered their services and charged a pretty penny for such knowledge. Joanna thought of the feast Saturday and sighed. Did she want to be stuck in the community all her life, eventually marrying a man who had little passion for anything in life? It was then Joanna made her decision. She would slip away during the barn dance on Saturday and go see David.

As the community was abuzz with the festivities at the dance on Saturday night, Joanna excused herself to go back to the house, hugging her brother and her father tightly before exiting, saying she felt ill and needed to call it an early night. Unnoticed by anyone else in the community, she then proceeded down the well-worn path and made her way to town. She made her way to the address David had scrawled on a ripped piece of an envelope from his coveralls and knocked on his door.

David opened the door, rubbing his eyes, apparently awakened by her rapping. He was groggy but smiled broadly in recognition. "Joanna, is that you are am I dreaming?"

"No. You're not dreaming, David. I'm really here." She paused a moment, considering her options. She thought for a moment about what advice her mother would give her in this moment. She thought back to when she was a little girl clutching on to her mother's skirt, frightened by some imaginary threat. She would have said, "Ah, my precious little girl, there is nothing to be afraid of but your own imagination. If you don't give your fear power over you, you can achieve anything you want in this lifetime." Joanna hesitated a moment then said to David all while blushing and smiling, "I came to be with you David, and hopefully one day be your wife."

David took Joanna by the hand and led her over his front stoop, making sure she didn't trip over the door sill on the way in. When he shut the door behind her he pulled her into his arms and kissed her deeply. Joanna felt a joy like none other she had felt in her life, spread through her bones and body. He then looked deeply into her eyes and said, "Well. I'm not the smartest man you will ever know, nor will I ever be the ideal of perfection, but I promise you this Joanna. I am a decent man with a good heart, and I promise to make this life the best we can possibly have together. So, yes. I do want you to stay with me. You're all I've thought about since I met you that day at the library, and you're all I want to think about for the rest of my days." The pair then walked hand in hand into David's modest living room where they sit side by side on the sofa, holding each other until they drifted off peacefully.

AMISH GOODNIGHT

GILLIAN BROWN

Chapter 1

Mary smiled, luxuriating in the warm sunlight as it danced across her pale skin, with her hand pressed firmly to her belly. Her normal Amish clothes had been traded-in for those which could easily accommodate a swelling stomach, and life felt purposeful and easy.

One of the beauties of Amish life, was the miracle of new birth. Yet, there were secrets around women's bodies within her community too. The older women often muttered around a female, prescribing all kinds of herbs and salves for whatever ailed her. Mary wanted to learn how to make these mysterious pastes, but was told quite pointedly that healing work was the business of older women, and she was far too young to take it on.

While English women held baby showers and gatherings before the birth of a new child, the Amish felt it best not to draw too much attention. After all, being in the spotlight was a form of pride. That, of course, and there was the fact that someone within her community was almost always with-child. Birthing did not carry the same stigmas in her world as it did in the English one.

Amish women would regularly work right up until the hour of their child's delivery. The lack of television and modern media meant that all the women had little to no exposure to the fact that many modern women feared the pain of birth, as well as complications during labor.

Within their communities there were significantly lower incidences of caesarian births, as well as pregnancy complications. Instead, they were surrounded by stories about easy childbirth and knew that labor was simply a normal part of life. New life was not something to be feared or even celebrated to excess. Instead, this was a mere fact of life.

Mary breathed deeply. Her husband Jacob should have been home already, but it wasn't terribly unusual for him to be late, especially since the busy season for their store was approaching. He was probably still building a shed or a shelf, toiling in the carpentry area of the shop, or maybe even huddled down, intently designing a crib for their new arrival.

Granted, Mary was only a few weeks along, but Jacob had been delighted when she'd told him the news. Like most Amish men, he'd been dreaming of having a son since he was a teenager. The idea that it might finally come to pass this year was a notion that swelled his heart with pride. A boy would be able to carry on the family name and traditions. Jacob would be able to pass on his carpentry skill set, and would grow old knowing their Amish lineage was secure.

Jacob was a simple man, who typically didn't want much from life. His parents, aunts, and uncles had helped the young couple to build their own store, which their community had cobbled together near the highway. There, they sold canned goods, vegetables, and other items made from wood like sheds and furniture.

Mary had been moved beyond words when Jacob's father had presented them the deed to their land. The rise in the cost of land in the English world had meant that so many of the Amish had no choice but to sell off their farms and move to Indiana where prices were significantly cheaper.

Lancaster county Pennsylvania had become impossibly expensive. The English world was one where capitalism reigned supreme, which meant that the Amish were left fumbling to try and preserve a way of life that was quickly going extinct.

Young couples who'd worked at manual labor their entire lives could no longer afford to buy even a few acres of land when they became of age. Yet, their culture was based-off farming and living off the land.

The Amish within her sect were never city dwellers, and so the availability of land had become a real problem. Many of the Amish had been forced into bankruptcy, which their preacher had referred to as another of the devil's works. After all, only in an evil society would good and hard-working folks fall so far behind.

Yet, the Amish way was one of peace. There would be no demonstrations to try and change the English world or reduce the surrounding s of land. There would be no complaints about the sheer unfairness of it all as they were being pushed out of their communities by the new high cost of living. They'd simply pray together and ask that God help them find a way.

As a result of the new market, Amish families now routinely banded together to help fund one another's land. The older generation understood that without their help, many young people would have no choice but to leave the Amish forever or starve on farms which yielded little crops because of poor location and over-farmed land. In order to survive, they had to band together.

The roadside store had been a great idea, and Mary and Jacob had been lucky. Their small plot of land was near the highway, and so the English were constantly driving by. Their curiosity about the Amish way of life made them want to stop in for cookies and pies—something Mary was happy to provide. Very often, they'd offer her bits of news about the outside world, information she both feared and relished.

The English would pull up in their expensive vans and cars, and most of them would stroll through the many aisles lining the store, searching for relics of the past. Things like—a handmade jam that tasted just like their grandma used to make, or a pie from one of the bakery shelves cooked with fresh ingredients that were now hard to find elsewhere and attention to detail. Marionberry pies were one of their biggest sellers.

These small comforts had drastically increased in value ever since the English world's pace had made the production of these goods virtually impossible. Only the

Amish were willing to spend seven hours churning a vat of honey butter. Good food required incredible patience, and from what Mary knew of the English world, things were dreadfully rushed in that way of life. Women were too busy holding down jobs to tend to their children, to teach them weaving and carpentry. Yet, for Mary's Amish sect, modernity was the enemy of virtue.

Like virtually everyone else in her community, Mary had enjoyed her Rumpspringa and had used every moment of her experimental life among the English to explore new things, and food was one of her top priorities.

Years ago, in a hospital, while visiting her dying grandfather she'd caught a few glimpses of a food magazine. Her entire life up until that point had consisted of her mother's simple yet delicious cooking. She knew nothing of food brought from faraway places like India and Asia, and she wanted to try them. Whatever money she'd been able to pocket during her break from the Amish, had gone towards small meals in restaurants and grocery stores. She'd been able to try fondue, and Paella, sushi and so much more. If she'd only had more time, perhaps she'd have been able to experience the nuances of French cuisine dancing across her palate. Yet, so many of the things she'd wanted to try had evaded her for lack of funds.

The experience was slightly marred, by the difficulties she and the other Amish teenagers had in surviving. Part of the Rumspringa ritual within her sect was that parents were meant to let go of their children so that they could explore the English world, first hand. With only twenty dollars in her pocket, Rumspringa also represented the worst possibilities of leaving the safety of her Amish community—like homelessness and a life of poverty.

Mary had banded together with a few friends and they'd all managed to obtain low paying jobs at a few nearby fast food joints, but the bills piled up higher and higher as all of them had fallen further and further behind. All of them were used to hard work, but at least within their small community, they'd work hard during the day and then come home to a safe place where they could eat and rest. Having menial jobs outside of the Amish community and having to pay for everything from food to high rent prices meant that staying afloat was almost impossible. Mary, as well as all of her friends had chosen to return back to their small Amish sect. Life in the English world was too hard.

Still, there were little things which had stayed with her from her time out in the English world. Mary had ripped one of the pages from a food and wine magazine and had stuffed it away in her apron. Each night, after finishing her chores, she often snuck away to the outhouse with a candle and sat in the darkness, just staring at the photograph, picking the various elements of the food apart. The English somehow even made a show of eating—and yet this was also a form of art. Not everything on an English plate was meant to be eaten, which was a novel concept to Mary. Some foods were garnish—which meant that they were intended only for show. The concept seemed wasteful to Mary, but also endlessly intriguing.

Mary pressed her hand to her belly again and reached down to grab a clothes pin. The wind rustled through the already- hanging sheets and she felt a strange wave of gratitude rush through her body. There was so much suffering in the world...but somehow, she had at least been born into a peaceful community. The Amish had problems, but at least they faced them together.

As Mary turned to go inside, at once, she saw him standing in the middle of her doorway wearing a black slack-vest.

Her heart thumped rapidly as she strained to take in the seriousness of the situation. It seemed totally impossible—like something out of a nightmare, that there would be a strange man in her house. Then, Mary saw it—a small handgun which was cocked and poised at the ready, aimed directly at her head.

The handgun was now aimed at the middle of her temple and his bloodshot eyes were filled with rage. Mary screamed and ducked, trying desperately to flee as the first blast cut through the air. Then, she ran right into her drying white sheets, tripping over her own feet as she covered the white linen in a huge amount of her blood.

She could hear the clop of his heavy boots as he descended from the porch, and walked over to where she lay in the yard. He seemed to be some kind of experienced killer and his lethality was evident in his bearing.

In the span of just a few seconds, a million thoughts raced through Mary's mind. Was he ex-Amish? Was a former customer from the store? She strained to try and place his face. There was something distantly familiar about him, but it was difficult to place him.

There was so much hardness and anger scrawled across his features that he looked more animal than human. Had the English world really become that hate-filled and dangerous? At that moment, Mary pitied him. She felt no anger towards him in her heart or soul. The man was obviously suffering, and what he needed was compassion and love.

She looked down at her stomach with a trembling hand. Blood was gushing out of the wound in her belly, and she felt panicked for the life of her unborn child. If God could only spare one of them; she hoped he'd somehow create a miracle to save her child, even though she was only a few weeks along.

The shooter was standing right over her now—the barrel of the gun, aimed at her temple. "Why?" Mary asked softly. "Do you even have a reason?" She asked again. She wasn't used to speaking to men so forcefully, but for some reason the words came out in a way she hadn't expected. The shooter paused for a moment, and then started to laugh at her snide remark.

Mary gripped at her stomach again. Maybe there was a chance to save the baby. "Don't do that!" The man screamed in a rage and Mary raised her hands out in front of her abdomen, defensively. "I'm sorry," she said. "It's just that if you kill me, these will be the last moments I ever share with my baby and I want him to feel loved." Her words made the man crack.

He lowered the gun and walked a few feet away from her and started to pace, talking to himself. Mary pressed one of the sheets to her stomach. She could feel contractions coming on now and was praying to God that she wouldn't miscarry.

"I keep screwing everything up!" The man shouted. Then he punched her white picket fence, accidentally driving a huge splinter into his knuckle. He screamed a few obscenities and started to kick the wall. Mary watched him for a moment, considering if he was far enough away that she might be about to flee. Then, she looked down. Even if her legs were able to carry her fast enough to escape his grasp, he might shoot her from behind. Plus, the twinge of contractions meant that she should try and remain as still as possible.

For some reason, the man's rage reminded Mary of her younger brother Noah. Whenever he'd burst into a fit of rage, her mother would cradle him close, kiss him on the forehead and sing him a song. Mary looked over at the distressed man, tears now streaming down his face. He ran a few muscled knuckles through his hair. Mary swallowed. "Do you want some pie?" Mary asked.

The idea seemed absurd. She didn't even know if she could walk, let alone hobble into the kitchen to retrieve a slice of pie, yet she decided to try. She groaned as she struggled to her feet, still bleeding, and went back into her house where she pulled out two white plates that clattered as she removed them gently from the cupboard. The shooter followed her inside and sat down while she placed a huge hunk of cherry pie in front of him with a weak grin.

Very slowly, the shooter picked up a fork and began to eat. Then, even more slowly, he began to talk.

He felt that the Amish had things too easy. He'd been laid off and had lost his health insurance. After his health coverage had been laid to ruin, his wife could no longer afford her dialysis treatments for kidney failure. She'd died while they were in the process of applying for state coverage. He'd written many letters of complaint to his senators, to the hospital that had denied treatment, and even to the governor, but they'd walled him off at every turn.

While drowning in that process, he'd lost all faith in mankind and had somehow gone rogue.

He'd managed to find out that the kidney transplant, which would have gone to his wife had instead been given to an elderly Amish person on medical assistance.

Mary slid a second piece of pie across the table. She watched as the man picked it up, breaking the crust off in his hand and putting it into his mouth.

"So, you blame the Amish for her death?' Mary asked. The shooter had put the gun down on the table flat as he considered his response. "I blame the system," the man said, looking up. "I blame the eighty-five-year-old who decided to take up a spot on the transplant list." Mary nodded silently. "You think that a person of advanced age should just be life to die?" Mary wanted to know. "When there aren't enough kidneys to go around, I do," he said softly, breaking off another chunk of pie, and swallowing. "It's an evil system," the man blurted out.

Mary cleared her throat. "Which system? The English system, or the Amish person that also needed help?" The man collapsed into a pile of sobs at the table, his hand shaking as it gripped the gun.

Just then, Mary heard the small bell which doubled as a door chime and she turned to see her husband Jacob step inside. She could clearly see the shock evident on his face as he took in the crazed man at the table and Mary's bleeding stomach. With a howl of anguish, Jacob ran towards the man at the table who now stood to meet the threat. Jacob lunged for his throat, but the man was quick with the handgun.

The sound of the blast rang out loudly and Mary fell to the floor, helpless to stop the horror around her. Before passing out from blood loss, Mary whispered a heartfelt prayer and hoped that God was listening.

Chapter 2

One year later.

Mary sat rocking the small bundle in her arms and listening to the soft cooing noises of her beautiful baby. After seven long months of bed rest and deep grief over the premature death of her beloved husband, Mary had finally given birth to a healthy baby girl. Several weeks early, the child had been small, but now little four-month-old Hope was just as happy and healthy as any other child in their Amish community.

Mary had feared losing both husband and child throughout her pregnancy despite the community's assurance to put her faith in God. She still trusted in his plan for her life, but at times she feared her own grief and fears would overwhelm her. Jacob had given his life to the gunman in order to save her and their baby. She only wished that he could have seen Hope grow up. Jacob would have made a wonderful father.

The gunman, in his remorse and grief had taken his own life that day in their kitchen, and Mary struggled daily with the amount of tragedy suffered on that horrible day. In addition to that, the Amish were beginning to whisper about the fact that she had not yet found a new husband to act as a father to Hope. To them, prolonged grief was sinful. Yet, Mary was beyond caring about the opinions of gossips. She needed to move slowly back into her life.

A soft knock on the door pulled Mary from her memories and she stood slowly, not wanting to wake the baby. The community had drawn together to help Mary throughout the past year and she opened the front door expecting one of the neighbors with a meal. Instead, she came face to face with a ghost from her past.

Mary drew in a startled breath as she stared at the man she had been promised to marry before Jacob. She could feel herself blush as she peered at his handsome chiseled features. Benjamin had been her first love and even now she could feel her heart flutter just at the sight of him. His deep set brown eyes and dark hair accented his strong jaw line, and even through his shirt she could see the outline of his abdominal muscles and biceps.

"Hello Benjamin, this is an unexpected surprise," Mary said softly. She invited him inside and felt her heart flutter when he agreed. Mary had heard that Benjamin was moving back into the community, but she hadn't realized it would happen so soon. She laid Hope into her bassinet and poured Benjamin a cup of Dutch tea from the kitchen.

She had so many questions to ask him, but was unsure of how to approach them. Benjamin had been one of the few teenagers not to return from his Rumspringa and the community had been devastated, including Mary. They were supposed to have been married the following fall. When Benjamin had not returned, Mary was left to deal with the loss in silence. The Amish did not talk about those who strayed from the faith. It was simply as though the person had never existed.

Instead of Benjamin, Mary had instead married Jacob and had quickly become pregnant. Now, for the second time in her life she was without a husband. Only this time, she had a baby to care for as well.

Benjamin took the glass of tea politely and took a seat when offered. Mary was just as pretty as he remembered and he was glad to be home. For three years, he had run from his people, his home, and his faith. When word finally got to him of Mary's predicament he knew it was time to stop running at last.

It had not been easy to earn his place back among the Amish, but now that he was here, he intended to fulfill his obligation and affection for Mary. "I hope you can forgive me the sins I committed against you when I was just an ignorant boy," Benjamin said. His voice was deeper now, and he spoke with such command that it made Mary blush. Mary paused for a moment. "There is nothing to forgive, Benjamin. You had every right to choose your own way."

Benjamin stayed for an hour reminiscing on times past and conversing lightly about the present. He found out that Mary had been unable to work during the later parts of her pregnancy (after the gun wound) and had been living solely off the support of the community. Now that she had given birth and both she and Hope were healthy, she would be required to return to her duties. With no father and husband, Mary's life would be difficult within the community to say the least.

Benjamin offered to come by the next day and help with the yard work and Mary gratefully accepted. A pain of guilt coursed through his body as he looked at Mary's smiling face. If not for his mistakes and choices, Mary would have been his wife, and Hope his child. Their suffering was in part because of him and he did not know how to ask forgiveness for such an offense.

With a slight nod of his head, Benjamin excused himself and promised to return in the morning. His eyes lingered for several more seconds on Mary's face, as he studied her features intently. Then, he turned to walk the mile back to his house.

After so many years away from his culture, the walk felt revitalizing in many ways. The feel of the fresh air against his face and the smell of grass brought back the joyous feelings he associated with his childhood. His life had not been easy since leaving the community and in many ways, he wished he had never left.

No matter what had happened in his time away, Benjamin always knew that this was where his heart lay. Here with his people, amongst family and friends and a way of life that brought peace. More than any of that though was the woman who still tugged upon his heart, calling him home. In the English world, he'd laid awake so many nights thinking about her, longing for her touch. None of the girls he'd met could compare to her kindness of virtue. For some reason, Mary was the standard by which Benjamin measured every other female.

Mary awoke the next morning, and after feeding and changing Hope she went to work baking fresh biscuits. By the time Benjamin arrived, the smell of breakfast was wafting along the morning breeze. She opened the door with a smile and offered Benjamin an invitation to eat with her. She was pleasantly grateful when he agreed.

As much as Mary had loved Jacob and been committed to him in every way, a part of her heart had always belonged to Benjamin and she couldn't help but notice those feelings blossom again when he was around. Their hands brushed for a moment as she handed him a platter of biscuits and her heart fluttered. Benjamin had let his fingertips linger on hers, at that made her core flood with a new sense of want. Benjamin smiled at her over the table and she felt safe for the first time in a long while.

After breakfast, Benjamin excused himself and went to work in the yard. The community had done much for Mary and Hope, but there were still many things that needed repairs and maintenance. Several of the fence posts needed to be reset and painted and their small vegetable field was in need of rotation.

Mary watched Benjamin work throughout the morning and carried him a fresh glass of tea to keep him cool while he labored in the sun. She set Hope down on a blanket smiling at the beautiful miracle in her midst. Hope was a joyful baby who rarely cried and Mary could clearly see a lot of Jacob in Hope's eyes, which was a reminder to her that he'd always be with her.

Occasionally Mary would glance up and see Benjamin staring back at her while he worked, and she wondered what his intentions might be, now that he had returned. There was a part of her that was very happy he had come back, but another part of her felt as though she were betraying Jacob in some way.

There were so many answers she still didn't have, but at the very least she was glad that Benjamin had found his way home. Benjamin jumped down from the she'd roof and made his way over to baby hope, where he easily scooped her into his strong arms. He tossed her up and down as she giggled. The scene made Mary's heart swell.

After Benjamin finished for the morning he said a quiet goodbye to Mary and Hope and headed out to do his own work for the day. He had agreed to work for his father's furniture business in the afternoons, making rocking chairs and cabinets. Building furniture had been one of the reasons Benjamin had left the Amish in the first place and he was glad to be back where his work was appreciated.

Benjamin had wanted to work in the English world making lots of money building and selling his own furniture, but none of his goals had worked the way he wanted them too.

Finding buyers who wanted handmade furniture in the English world was near to impossible. Benjamin would spend hours carving the intricate designs into his hand-crafted furniture piece by piece, only to find that a store down the street could produce a hundred pieces an hour for half the cost. The English frequented stores like Walmart and Ikea, where furniture was sold in droves.

No matter how many times Benjamin had explained that his quality of work was far superior to the manufactured furniture from the assembly lines, no one cared. He'd felt beaten down by the fact the that quality of his work didn't mean much in the English world.

Occasionally he would sell a single piece to an individual which would give him enough money to eat for a week or so, but there were many times when he went hungry as well. There were so many times when Benjamin had wanted to come home and resume his life in a place that appreciated his value, but his pride had stood in the way.

When he had learned of Mary's marriage to Jacob, he had seen no reason not to swallow his pride in order to return. Mary had always been the love of his life.

Now that Mary was alone, and raising a baby on her own, Benjamin knew the time had come for him to atone and make amends. In his heart, he had never stopped loving Mary and he could see that she still carried feelings for him too. He also knew that Mary had truly loved Jacob, and that the man had died defending her and their baby.

Benjamin was not looking to take Jacob's place in any way, he simply wanted to provide a good home and a proper future for Mary and Hope.

Throughout the next several months Benjamin and Mary resumed the friendship they had shared in their youth and Benjamin found the loneliness in his heart beginning to fade. When he held Hope in his arms, he felt alive in a way he had never before known, and when he peered into Mary's brown eyes he knew once again, the true meaning of peace.

One evening, he'd stayed on late at the farm and had goaded Mary into a dance with him. They were standing on the front porch, which was drenched in moonlight, and she'd never looked so beautiful. How could he not touch her? Ever so slowly, he'd placed his hands around her waist as they'd began to sway as Jacob sang her an old tune. When the song was over and they'd peeled their bodies apart, his heart was pounding a million times per minute. He felt so full of love that he feared he might burst. In the heat of the moment, he'd reached for her and had pressed his lips against hers.

Instead of pulling away, she had responded by draping her arms around his neck. "I love you Benjamin Johnson," he heard her whisper. He responded by kissing her on the cheek. "I've loved you since the first day I saw you," he said in his gruff voice. Then, from inside the small cottage Hope has started to cry. Benjamin watched in disbelief as Mary hurried away to tend to her child.

Chapter 3

Every morning Benjamin came and worked to help Mary establish herself once again and every afternoon he went to work making furniture for his father. He wanted nothing more than to make the arrangement permanent but he was afraid that Mary would not accept. After all, he'd broken her heart so many years ago. How could she ever learn to trust him again?

There were things about his life outside of the Amish community he had not shared with her as of yet, and he wondered if she would be able to accept him once she found out the truth. If he were to be a true husband to her and a good father to Hope, he would have to share that part of himself. It would not be fair of him to ask Mary to marry him under false pretenses. He would have to come clean.

Mary waited patiently in the living room bouncing Hope softly on her lap. Benjamin had asked to see her again this evening after his work was done and she had accepted. Over the last several months since Benjamin's return, she had allowed herself to cautiously renew the friendship with him they had once shared.

At times, she could tell that he was willing to offer her more, but he seemed hesitant to ask. She herself was not sure that she was ready for the commitment once again. The loss of Benjamin once and then the loss of Jacob had damaged her in so many ways. She was not sure she was willing or even able to open her heart for another. If she were though, the thought of it being with Benjamin felt like the right choice.

Every time Mary watched Benjamin with Hope, she felt her heart soar as though maybe God was giving her back some of what she had lost. When Jacob had been killed a part of Mary had died as well and she felt as though she would never be able to love another. With Benjamin, she felt as though she were at least ready to try again.

Mary heard the knock on the door and stood letting Benjamin inside. She had prepared herself as best as possible for what she thought he was going to ask her—to marry.

Slowly, Benjamin entered the sitting room with a pale face. In his hand, he held his hat, and today he seemed unable to make eye contact as he sat across from her on the sofa, clearing his through. "I'm sure you know by now, Mary, that I have serious feeling for you." He seemed to tremble as he spoke. "Before I can ask if you'll accept my hand, I need to tell you something very important. I hope you'll be able to love me in spite of it."

Mary leaned back in her chair, listening intently. Tears seemed to swell up in Benjamin's eyes. "One of the ways I made a living in the English world as an orderly at the hospital." He swallowed, seeming to choke on his own statements. "When I learned that Jed's wife Rebekah was in need of a kidney, I made changes to the organ transplant list. That shooter's wife was still on the list—the insurance hadn't actually removed her. I did that. I killed her."

The words felt like daggers piercing her heart. "You took that man's wife off the kidney transplant list?" Mary repeated. Benjamin nodded. "I had access to many of the files. I switched some of the paperwork so that it would look like his wife had been dropped by her insurance company, when she actually had another 30 days left on it. I didn't know how serious it was. I didn't know that she's die as a result."

Rage pulsated through Mary's body. Beautiful sweet Benjamin hadn't been simply acting out of the kindness of his heart, but to ease a guilty conscience. He was the reason that the shooter's wife had died, and he was also the reason that her husband Jacob had been targeted. Mary let out a wail that could have woken the dead, and Benjamin rushed to his feet to catch her.

"Don't touch me!" She screamed. "Get your filthy hands off me!" Mary shouted. Yet, even with the knowledge that he'd committed a grave sin, his hands felt like butter on her skin. She could see the remorse in his eyes—and yet his horrible stupid decision has resulted in so much death.

Benjamin dropped to his knees. "Please Mary...please forgive me." He said through a veil of tears. He sobbed loudly and was drenching her shirt. Mary looked up and smacked him hard across the face. Benjamin flew back, stunned. "Go tell them what you've done. Go tell everyone what you've done, or I will!" Mary shrieked. Benjamin continued to hold tightly to her skirt while sobbing.

Then, suddenly he stood and turned to go. "You made me love you again," Mary blurted out. He turned to face her. "I never stopped loving you and I never will. "

Chapter 3

Benjamin did as he was told and reported his crime to the bishop who hen reported him to the English authorities. After two lengthy trials, he was found guilty of forgery and placed on probation—a status which destroyed his honor within the community, but he seemed to learn the many lessons that followed.

Despite it all, Benjamin wordless crept onto Mary's farm each morning and did the work—milking the cows and working the fields, before returning to his own. After the first month, he left her a small hand-made card, again begging for forgiveness.

He'd gone to the shooter's family too and had explained his part in what happened. Of course, he hadn't been responsible for the murderer's decision to pick up a gun and start killing people, but he had caused that man incredible pain by inadvertently causing the death of his wife. Slowly, months turned to years, and Mary was eventually able to see the Benjamin was sincere. He would spend the rest of his life trying to make amends if he had to.

About six months later, she'd invited him into the house for dinner again. "You can never lie to me or anyone else ever again," Mary had said, sipping on a glass of cool lemonade. "You can never be that person you became in the English world again, because that person was a monster." Mary said. She could already see tears streaming down Benjamin's face.

"Will it ever be possible for me to earn your love back? Will you ever be able to love me again?" Benjamin asked. "I never stopped loving you," Mary answered quietly "Not after you skipped out on our wedding, not after all the horrible things you've done. I have loved you through ever second of it."

Mary got up from the table, walked around it and sat down on his lap. Ever so slowly, she kissed the tears already wet on his face. "I thought that maybe if I came home, I could make things right," Benjamin muttered. "But when I came home you were the only thing I could see. You've always been my home, Mary. You're my very soul." "Then do right by me and do right by yourself. Forgiveness is not found in the words you speak, but the things you do."

Mary had been flabbergasted when Benjamin took it upon himself to help sick people. He registered as a donor and gave up one of his kidneys, as well as a significant amount of bone marrow. He was using his very body to make amends, and while he could never go back and undo his crime, he'd made sure that three different families were spared the grief of losing loved ones. The months rolled by and Mary could see the changes in him—that his mistakes had somehow deepened him and made him more human.

It was late in the evening when he'd come to her home, knocking on the door. She answered in her nightgown and he'd pulled her own into the cold night air, laughing. Then, he dropped to one knee. "Mary me," Benjamin blurted out. Mary approached him slowly. She undid the buttons on his shirt until they fell away, revealing the huge scar across his abdomen...one he'd earned from donating a kidney. Then, she unbuckled his belt and felt the scar on his thigh—earned from donating bone marrow twice. Then, Mary looked into his eyes. He'd been a foolish young man, but he was now someone new. Someone she could trust. But he was always someone she'd loved with all her heart. She loved him then, and she'd love him forever.

CALL OF THE AMISH

ELIZA FITZGERALD

Part One:

The call came in the middle of the night. Somehow Elizabeth King's daed had heard the telephone ringing in his shop, and had hurried from bed to answer it. He had the only phone for miles around, and often when the phone rang there was an emergency that needed tending to, though just as often someone from the community hurried to their house to use the phone as well.

"Elizabeth, wake up, my girl."

Elizabeth squinted into the sudden brightness, and for a moment she was so disoriented that she had no idea where she was or who was talking to her. Then she realized that her maemm was kneeling beside her bed with a kerosene lantern shining.

"What is it, Maemm?" Elizabeth asked.

"Your cousin, Melissa, she needs your help," her maemm replied. "Her babe is coming early, and there isn't enough time to get her to the birthing center that she chose in the city. She's refusing to go to the local hospital, and you're the only midwife she knows. Hurry now, and get dressed, girl. Your daed is getting the buggy ready to take you."

Elizabeth felt her eyes go wide and round as she drew in a sharp breath. Thoughts whirred through her mind as she slipped from beneath the covers of her bed, careful not to jostle her sister, Sarah, who grumbled in her sleep and turned toward the wall. As Elizabeth slipped into her dress and tucked her hair up into her kapp, she looked at her maemm.

"I don't know if I'm ready for this, Maemm," she whispered, feeling her stomach form into a tight knot.

"The Lord has delivered you to this point," her maemm said. "Pray that He will guide your work, and remember that all you do is in the glory of His name."

Elizabeth nodded, kissed her maemm on the cheek, and hurried down the stairs to get her shawl from where it hung on a peg by the front door. Her daed was already in the driver seat of the buggy, waiting in the moonlight to drive her quickly into town where her Englischer cousin was waiting for her.

As her daed drove along shadowy lanes, Elizabeth bowed her head, and silently prayed, *"Dear Lord, I am scared. I have never done this by myself before, and I need You to be with me. I need You to guide my hands. Please lift up Melissa and her unborn babe. Let me be an instrument of Your peace. Let me do this well, Lord. Please, oh, please. Amen."*

When she got done with her prayer, she clenched her fists together on her lap, pulling her shawl tighter around her shoulders. Elizabeth had never been so terrified of anything in her whole life, but at the same time she felt a sense of peace descend upon her. In that moment, she knew, she just knew that the Lord had heard her prayer. He had created her for this moment.

Her daed pulled the buggy up in front of Melissa's house, the electric laws all blazing, and Melissa's husband, Jim, on the front porch, pacing. When he caught sight of her, he jogged down the stairs, and put his arm around her. "Elizabeth! I'm so glad that you are here," Jim said. "She's saying that she's going to have the baby any moment."

"Did you get the items together that were on the birthing center's list?" Elizabeth asked, calmly.

Jim nodded, his head bobbing up and down. He looked so helpless that Elizabeth felt sorry for him. She shrugged out of her shawl and handed it to him. "Good," Elizabeth said, rolling up her sleeves. "Are you going to stay in the room? I'm sure that Melissa would find that helpful."

"Anything," Jim said. "Just tell me what I need to do, and I'll do it."

Taking a deep breath, Elizabeth walked into the bedroom where Melissa was moaning softly as she lay on the bed. With a quick glance at her cousin, all of Elizabeth's cool, collected calm seemed to flee. She murmured another quick prayer.

"Hello, cousin," Elizabeth said in a soft tone as she entered the darkened room. She paused to allow her cousin to register her appearance, but also to gauge the situation that lay before her. "Melissa," she continued in a firmer voice. "You are going to be just fine. I'm going to open these curtains to let in some light." Elizabeth wasn't sure why, but it felt right to let light in. Her mind flickered to one of her favorite Bible verses [something about letting your light shine]

When Elizabeth got closer to the bed, Melissa opened her eyes and reached out to grip Elizabeth's hand. "Thank you for coming," Melissa said through gritted teeth as another contraction ripped through her small body. "Lizzy, I don't know if I can do this."

Hearing her cousin call her by her childhood nickname brought Elizabeth soundly into the present, and a sense of peace descended on her. She reached out and smoothed her cousin's sweaty curls away from her forehead. "You can do this," she said. "And you will."

Part Two:

"It was the most amazing experience I've ever had, Paul," Elizabeth said with a contented sigh as she leaned back against the seat of Paul's buggy. She could still feel the rush of adrenaline that had coursed through her veins as Melissa pushed the baby girl out into Elizabeth's hands. When she had handed the baby to her cousin, tears had run rivulets down both of their cheeks. Jim had cut the cord, and beamed with the pride of a new father, though Elizabeth had caught the relief in his eyes too. He hadn't been able to stop thanking her.

"I just know that this is what God brought me into the world to do," she added. Then she turned to her beau, the boy she had grown up with, fallen in love with, and expected to marry as soon as he took over his daed's farm. She expected to see her own excitement reflected in his eyes; he had always been her biggest cheerleader, especially as she had embarked on her journey to become a midwife.

Instead, Paul gazed at her with serious eyes and his mouth drawn into a tight frown. "Elizabeth," he said, drawing out the syllables of her name as he often did when he thought she was being silly.

"What?" she asked, her eyebrows furrowing. She thought that Paul would have been excited for her. She thought he would have seen the importance of the event through her eyes. She had thought they had the same vision for their future. It seemed to her now that she thought wrong.

"God brought you into the world to be my wife," Paul said softly.

Elizabeth's confusion amplified. There was a buzzing in her ears that she didn't like. "God created me to be many things," she said, her breath feeling hollow in her chest.

"Of course," Paul said in a cajoling tone, but something in his expression made her think that he didn't believe that.

"You know that I can't wait to be your wife," Elizabeth said. "But the feeling I got delivering Melissa's baby, well, I can't even describe it. There are no words for being a witness to a miracle like that. Doing that over and over would be an amazing way to live."

Paul turned toward her in the carriage seat. He reached out to take her hands in his own. "Elizabeth, it's fine for you to do midwife work right now, but what happens after we get married? You'll have a household to run. And what happens when we begin to have children?"

The starkness of his words made Elizabeth pause. She knew that he had a point, and she wasn't going to disagree with him on that point. But she wasn't willing to concede that she should give up being a midwife just because her life would be busier.

Slowly she said, "I can't wait to have a home and children of our own, but I just can't see how being a midwife wouldn't be able to fit into that picture."

Paul pressed his lips together. "You'll simply be too busy." He said it in a tone that made it clear that he thought that was all there was to say on the matter, but that fact made Elizabeth even more upset.

"God doesn't just create us for one purpose," Elizabeth said. "I'm sorry, Paul, but I just don't think that I agree with you."

The look on Paul's face went from disapproving to impassive. Elizabeth had never seen him act like this before, and she didn't like it one bit. "I think you should take me home now," she said, drawing her hand away. Turning her face away from him, she pressed her lips together. If she said something now, she knew that there was a chance that she would say something that she would regret.

Paul didn't move for a long moment. So long, in fact that Elizabeth almost looked over at him, but instead she held firm. Finally he heaved a sigh, and flicked the reins. As the buggy moved off down the road, Elizabeth felt a rush of tears flood her eyes. Blinking rapidly so they wouldn't fall, she tried to figure out a way to make Paul understand where she was coming from, but her mind was a blank.

Instead she decided to pray. "*Dear Lord, I don't understand what is happening right now. Paul has always been my soul mate, the one that I know I'm destined to be with. And yet, today I know that You showed me another part of Your plan for me. How do I make Paul see this? How do I explain it? The feeling that delivering Melissa's baby gave me? Where are you leading me, Lord? Please show me the way. Amen.*"

When she finished praying, Elizabeth felt a sense of peace descend on her. She drew a deep breath, and said, "Paul, I don't know how to explain this feeling to you, but I know that what I did today came from God. I don't want things to be bad between us, but right now this is the path that He is leading me down. I...I think that we should spend a bit of time apart."

"How can you say that?" Paul asked with a gruffness in his voice that Elizabeth knew well. He did that when he was trying to keep the hurt at bay. She had never caused him pain before, and the realization made her heart ache. Yet she wasn't going to back off.

"I just know in my heart that if we're going to have a future together then we need to trust in the Lord and His plan for us," Elizabeth said.

Just as she finished speaking, the buggy turned into the drive for Elizabeth's house. When Paul reined the horse in, Elizabeth was quick to get out on her own. She hurried into the house without looking back. She needed to keep her resolve, and she knew that if she looked back, her heart might break.

Part Three:

"Gross-mammi? Can I talk to you?" Elizabeth leaned on the kitchen door jamb of her grandmother's house.

"Of course, dear," her gross-mammi said, glancing over her shoulder at her. She continued to mix the butter into the flour for the pie crust that she was making.

Elizabeth grabbed an apron off a hook on the wall as she entered the kitchen, and tied it around her waist. One of the rules about entering Gross-mammi's kitchen was that one had to help when they came in. No matter what. No matter who. Elizabeth had never minded. She found the act of baking with her grandmother soothing.

Reaching for a paring knife, Elizabeth began to slice strawberries for the berry pie her grandmother was preparing. "I delivered my cousin Melissa's baby yesterday," she said.

"Your daed told me," Gross-mammi said with a nod. "I'm proud of you, my girl. That's God's work."

Elizabeth felt a burst of joy in her chest. "I felt like God was touching my hands," she said, tears welling at the memory. "I can't think of a better way to describe it."

She finished cutting the strawberries, added them to the bowl with the blueberries and raspberries, and poured in a cup of sugar. As she was coating the berries her grandmother reached across the counter, and tapped her hand. Elizabeth glanced up at her beloved gross-mammi, and she could see the question in the older woman's eyes.

With a sigh, Elizabeth wiped her hands on her apron, and said, "I'm having a problem with Paul." As soon as she said the words, tears flooded her eyes. Unable to keep them in, they ran rivulets down her cheeks. Swiping at them with the heels of her hands, Elizabeth slumped over the counter, leaning her elbows on the floury surface.

"Oh, is that all?" Gross-mammi asked, waving her hand in the air. Elizabeth looked at her grandmother with surprise. The older woman continued, "A little lovers' spat, no?"

Elizabeth swiped at her leaky eyes again. "I don't know," she said unable to keep the misery out of her voice. "He doesn't like the idea of my being a midwife. At least not after we get married. If we get married, I guess. I just couldn't get him to understand how much I feel like God has called me to deliver babies, to be His hands in the world. Am I wrong, Gross-mammi?"

Her grandmother was silent, silent and still for a long time before she picked up the bowl of berries and poured them into the pie crust. Finally she said, "I think that only the Lord can answer that question, my dear. My advice to you is to pray. Pray hard, and then listen. Listen with all your heart and soul. If you do that, then I'm sure that you will find the answer that you seek."

Watching her grandmother put the pie into the oven, Elizabeth felt peace descend upon her. She knew that her gross-mammi's advice was sound and true. She did need to pray. And yet...right now she also needed her grandmother's comforting presence. And she needed pie.

"Is there any cleaning you need done, Gross-mammi?" Elizabeth asked. If she could distract herself by helping her grandmother, then she could perhaps calm her racing mind down enough to let her soul catch up. Then she could pray.

"Would you mind bringing down the rugs, and giving them a good beating?" Elizabeth was sure that she could see a smile hovering around her gross-mammi's mouth. The rugs probably didn't need to be beaten, but Elizabeth was glad for the opportunity to work out some of her frustration.

"Of course," Elizabeth said as she headed into the front room to get the first rug. Rolling it up, she hefted it over her shoulder.

Over and over, Elizabeth retrieved rug after rug, hung them on the clothesline, and beat the dust and dirt out of them. By the time she was done, she was exhausted and sweaty, but she also felt calmer. After she had placed the last rug back in the upstairs guest bedroom, Elizabeth jogged back down the stairs.

"All done, Gross-mammi," she called as she came into the kitchen.

"Just in time," her grandmother said. "The pie just came out of the oven. Come, sit with me, and we'll have a slice."

"Great," Elizabeth said with a grin.

The two women sat together, and for a long stretch of time Elizabeth felt soothed, which was exactly what she had hoped to feel when she came here. But then thoughts of Paul started to creep back in. By the time she was taking her last bite of pie, she was having trouble swallowing. As if her gross-mammi could read her thoughts, she reached over and patted Elizabeth's hand again.

"Just remember to pray," Gross-mammi said. "The Lord will give you all the answers that you need. Just a moment." Elizabeth threaded her hands together as she watched her grandmother leave the room. A moment later she returned with a large Bible in her hands.

Opening it, she said, "I think this will help you. Ecclesiastes 3: 1-8, 'To every thing there is a season, and a time to every purpose under the heaven 2 A time to be born, and a time to die; a time to plant, and a time to pluck up that which is planted;3 A time to kill, and a time to heal; a time to break down, and a time to build up;4 A time to weep, and a time to laugh; a time to mourn, and a time to dance;5 A time to cast away stones, and a time to gather stones together; a time to embrace, and a time to refrain from embracing;6 A time to get, and a time to lose; a time to keep, and a time to cast away;7 A time to rend, and a time to sew; a time to keep silence, and a time to speak;8 A time to love, and a time to hate; a time of war, and a time of peace.'"

"I've always liked that one," Elizabeth agreed. As she kissed her grandmother goodbye, Elizabeth felt calm once again. She needed to pray.

Part Four:

Dear Lord, Elizabeth prayed as she walked toward her closest friend, Miriam's, house. *I know that You are the designer of my life. I want to trust in the path that You have laid out for me. I believe, Lord, help me in my unbelief. I know that I am a sinner, and that I try to assert my own will instead of listening to You. I want to change, though, Lord. I ask you to show me what path You want for me. Should I be a midwife? Or should I marry Paul? Or...Lord, I know that it is asking a lot, but is there a way that I could have both? I'm listening, Lord. Show me the way. Amen.*

Elizabeth swallowed as she finished her prayer. It wasn't that prayer was foreign to her; she prayed often and with fervent sincerity. She had meant what she had prayed, that she was a sinner who all too often tried to fit her will onto that of the Lord's. But she had also meant her plea for help. Now she had to clear her head—and heart—to listen and hear the Lord's answer.

By the time she got to Miriam's house, Elizabeth still felt as confused as ever. She couldn't help feeling like she wanted to press the Lord for an answer right now, but she knew all that would get her was a lesson in being patient.

"Elizabeth!"

Miriam clattered down the front steps, and threw her arms around Elizabeth. For a moment all of her stress melted away as she hugged her friend back. This was what she needed, desperately. Perhaps that was why she had felt such an overwhelming desire to visit Miriam today. The thought occurred to her so fast that Elizabeth almost missed it. Maybe this was the Lord answering some part of her prayer. Maybe she needed to listen to what Miriam had to say. Miriam had gone through more in her young life than most people would in all their years so Elizabeth definitely trusted her friend's perspective.

"My maemm told me that you delivered your cousin's baby," Miriam said. "How wonderful! Come sit in the garden, and I'll go get some lemonade and cookies. You'll have to tell me all about it."

Elizabeth smiled, feeling relief wash over her. "Let me help," she said.

With a firm shake of her head, Miriam said, "Go sit in the garden. You're my guest. Let me get the refreshments."

Knowing that it was futile to argue with Miriam, Elizabeth headed toward the garden as her friend went to the house. Miriam and her family lived on the edge of their small town on a large farmette. Miriam's daed owned a popular furniture shop that was busy with tourists all through the summer months.

Chickens scattered as Elizabeth crossed the stone path toward the large kitchen garden that Miriam's maemm had spent years cultivating. Elizabeth sat down at the small wicker table set under a big willow tree. A moment later Miriam joined her.

Setting the lemonade and cookies under the tree, Miriam said, "So, tell me all about it. How was it delivering a baby for the first time?"

"It was beyond anything I can even explain," Elizabeth said, feeling a rush of pleasure as she remembered the experience. "It was like...like I was actually the Hands of God. Like He was guiding all my movements. I loved every second of it. I can't wait to do it again." Her smile faded as she thought about Paul.

"What's wrong?" Miriam asked, clearly seeing her friend's sudden distress.

Elizabeth sighed. "Paul wasn't very happy with my first experience."

"Why not?" Miriam held out the plate of cookies toward Elizabeth.

"He doesn't think that I can do both midwifery and being his wife," she said.

"Did he propose?" Miriam asked around a mouthful of cookie, her eyes widening.

Shaking her head, Elizabeth said, "No. I'm sure he's going to one day. Probably sooner rather than later, but he might not since he doesn't like the idea of my being a midwife. I wish that I could make him understand that what I'm doing when I deliver babies is God's work. I don't feel like it would detract from my duties as his wife."

Miriam bit into another cookie, and tipped her head to one side as she appeared to consider the situation. Elizabeth sucked in her breath as she waited to hear what her friend thought. What if Miriam felt the same way as Paul? That would only add to her confusion. The suspense grew as the silence stretched, and Elizabeth felt a knot tighten in her stomach.

Finally Miriam said, "I'm sure that Paul feels scared."

Her words shocked Elizabeth for a moment. Then she furrowed her brow, and said, "What do you mean?"

Taking a sip of her lemonade, Miriam shrugged. "It seems pretty clear to me. God has given you an incredible gift. You've found your calling. Most people wait their entire lives to find their calling. Paul has thought of you as his calling for your whole lives. To be married to you is what he is called to do."

"I always thought that too," Elizabeth said softly. "And I still do. I just wonder...can't God call us to more than one thing."

"Of course," Miriam said, waving her hand in the air. "There is a season for everything, so why can't we have more than one calling in our lives."

"My gross-mammi said almost the exact same thing," Elizabeth said. "I just wish that I could make Paul understand that."

"Maybe it's not so much about making Paul understand, but putting the situation entirely in God's hands," Miriam said.

"What do you mean?" Elizabeth wiped the cookie crumbs off her skirt as she looked at her friend.

"Well, you just need to do your best at what God is asking of you right now," Miriam said. "Paul needs to do the same. When the Lord is ready for the two of you to be together, you will be."

"You're so smart," Elizabeth told her friend. "I knew there was a reason that I wanted, no, needed, to come here today."

Miriam grinned at her. "You know I'm always here to help you if you need it," she said.

Elizabeth squeezed her friend's hand. She did know, and more than that she knew that the Lord had given her such a friend just for situations like this. She whispered a quick prayer of thanks before she reached for another cookie.

Part Five:

"I don't understand why you won't come out with me today," Paul said.

Looking at him as he stood at the bottom of the porch steps made Elizabeth's heart ache, but she had to keep in mind the advice that Gross-mammi and Miriam had given her. She had to follow God's plan for her, and she needed to stay strong on that. If that didn't mean that Paul was a part of that right now, then she needed to accept that and be strong.

"Because there's a baby over at the Hoestetler homestead that needs to be delivered," Elizabeth explained.

Paul frowned up at her. "I thought you had decided not to do midwifery anymore."

"Jean is one of my very best friends. You know that. Of course I need to be there." Elizabeth returned Paul's frown. The ache in her heart increased and stole her breath. Why would God let her feel so much pain? Cause so much pain between the two of them? Elizabeth knew that He was a good and loving God, so why would it be that He would allow such heartache to exist in the world?

And yet, Elizabeth knew that pain existed because of the sin of Adam and Eve. She was a sinner, so why should she expect any special treatment? "Paul," she said in a soft voice, "I truly believe that this is what God is calling me to do right now. I can't say if this is what God will always ask me to do, and I do think that you and I are called to be together, but I need to answer His call."

Paul's frown deepened, but he didn't argue with her. Instead he seemed to be listening to what she had to say. Finally he asked, "So what does that mean for us right now?"

"Right now?" Elizabeth repeated. She could sense the hurt in Paul, and she thought of what Miriam had said. If he was hurting as much as she was, then she didn't want to make it worse. "I think it means that we both need to pray deeply, and listen with all our hearts to what the Lord is telling us. Then we follow His plan, His path, His will for our lives. When it's time for us to come back together, He will let us know."

Paul nodded. "Can I still come to see you every Sunday?" he asked in a cracking voice that shattered Elizabeth's voice.

"Of course," she said. "And we'll keep talking about where God is leading us."

Elizabeth tried hard to put the whole conversation with Paul out of her mind as she delivered Sarai's baby that afternoon. Her good friend Jean helped, but seemed nervous to be attending her own sister's labor. After the little boy had been placed safely in his mother's arms, Elizabeth sank into a sofa in the parlor. Jean brought her a glass of tea and a muffin.

Jean sat down on a chair nearby, and the two of them ate in contented silence. When they were done, Elizabeth said, "I definitely know that God is leading me down this path right now."

The curious look on Jean's face made Elizabeth giggle, though she suspected that she was really just very tired. Elizabeth explained, "I've been praying that God would show me my path in life. I feel called to two such paths actually. Being a midwife is what I'm supposed to do right now, but I know that one day I'll marry Paul. I think that he is finally starting to understand that we can't impose our will on God's plans for us."

"That's not something we can ever do, is it?" Jean said.

"The thing that really bothers me about the whole situation," Elizabeth said, "is that Paul is so hurt by it all, and that's truly not what I want."

"You aren't hurting him on purpose," Jean said as if this was a fact that was obvious. "Unfortunately God's plan, if you truly want to submit to His will, bypasses all other plans."

"I know," Elizabeth agreed. "But do you suppose that there is a way to lessen his pain?"

Jean considered the question. "I'm sure that you are already doing it, but I would advise you to pray. Pray hard and listen hard."

Elizabeth nodded seriously. "I have been, and I'll continue to do it."

"Do you think that God is asking you to take some part away from each other for a while?" Jean asked.

The adrenaline from the delivery was wearing off, leaving Elizabeth with a bone deep exhaustion setting in. "No, I don't think that at all," she said.

"So, can't you just keep spending time together? And when it's time for the two of you to get married, you'll just know," Jean suggested.

"I guess I hadn't really thought about that," Elizabeth said with a frown. "That seems quite stupid of me, doesn't it?"

Jean shrugged. "Sometimes the most obvious solutions evade us."

"My biggest problem is that I don't know if Paul will feel the same way," Elizabeth said. "He's been so hurt by my midwifery."

"Maybe he just needs time to get used to it," Jean said. "You've just started. How many babies have you delivered so far?"

"Just two," Elizabeth said.

"Then time will help him accept this part of your life," Jean said firmly.

Elizabeth felt better as soon as Jean spoke. "You know, Jeannie, you are so smart."

Jean grinned at her. "I know," she replied. "But thanks that's nice of you to say."

As Elizabeth sank back into the sofa and felt her eyes drift closed, she offered up a prayer of thanks to the Lord that He had given her such good friends and advisors. How did she deserve such good things?

Part Six:

Three more babies were delivered in the next three weeks, and Elizabeth felt more certain than ever that God had called her to be a midwife. Things between her and Paul had been different, but not as bad as she had feared. Though he had been visiting less often, the visits that they did have seemed better to her. If pressed, she wasn't sure she would have been able to say exactly what seemed better, though there were little signs that Paul was beginning to understand how much being a midwife meant to her.

So when Paul pulled up the driveway in a new buggy, Elizabeth felt her heart stir with excitement and delight. She came out onto the porch as he jumped down. "What do you think?" he asked with an easy grin that she hadn't seen in weeks.

"It's lovely," she said. "When did you get it?"

"Yesterday," Paul said. He was happy, his eyes crinkling in the corners. There was a giddy energy coming off of him that reminded her of a child. "Can you come for a ride? Right now?"

Elizabeth laughed. She couldn't help it. He looked so happy. "Let me just grab my shawl."

Paul helped her up into the buggy. "Isn't it roomy?" he asked when they were both settled.

Glancing at the back seat, Elizabeth nodded. "It's great. It must have cost you a fortune," she said.

"I've been saving for it for a while," Paul admitted. "Actually I was praying that God would show me the right time to buy it, and recently I felt that it was time."

"I'm glad," Elizabeth said. She felt a momentary flash of surprise and disappointment that she wasn't included in the decision making process. Then she realized that Paul was doing exactly what she had asked him to do. He was listening for God's will in his life just as she had been doing in hers. The part of her that had felt so jealous of his decision a moment before suddenly rejoiced in it.

"It's big for a good reason," Paul was saying. Elizabeth realized with a guilty start that she hadn't been paying attention as he waxed lyrical about the many wonderful features of the buggy, which she was sure was top of the line. Paul probably had a reason for every choice that he had made; that was one of the many qualities that she loved about him.

"Oh?" Elizabeth said.

He nodded, and gave her a smile even as they lapsed into silence. They drove to the top of the highest hill in the county. The two of them had been coming here since they had first started courting, and Elizabeth still felt it was the most romantic place she could ever imagine.

As Paul pulled the horse to a stop, he half turned on the bench seat so that he was mostly facing her. "My maemm told me that you delivered another baby yesterday," he said. "How is that going?"

Elizabeth couldn't keep the surprise from her face as she said, "Amazing. It's still amazing."

Paul was quiet for such a long time that Elizabeth thought that he might be trying to come up with yet another way to talk her out of continuing to pursue being a midwife. Then he ran a hand along the back of his neck. "I'm sorry," he said. "I was wrong to try to stop you from doing something that you are so obviously meant to do. The truth is, well, the truth is that I was scared. I was scared that if you found something that was more important than me that I might lose you forever."

Miriam and Jean had been spot on with their assessment of the situation. Elizabeth reached across the seat to take Paul's hand. "I'm sorry that I didn't stop to listen to you and your concerns," she said. "I mean, really listen. The way you deserved."

"That's partly my fault. I was so blinded by my fears that I pressed you for something that I had no right to ask. I should have been listening to the Lord first, and then talking to you about everything in a calm and open manner," Paul said.

"Thank you for that," Elizabeth said. "But I think that what I should have said is that I understand that change can be scary, but also that I don't think God gives us just one calling in our lives. I think that He calls us to different things throughout our lives."

"That's a faithful thought," Paul said.

"Miriam planted that seed for me. I've been praying about it for weeks, and I see that the more I pray and listen, the more paths I can see that God is leading me down," Elizabeth said.

"God does call us down many paths," Paul agreed. "I see that now."

"I'm glad," Elizabeth said.

"And that's why I bought this buggy," Paul said.

Elizabeth's eyebrows knit together in confusion. "What do you mean?"

"This buggy is big enough for a family," Paul said. "I've been praying about it for a while now, and I felt led to buy it now."

"Paul, what are you saying?" Elizabeth asked as her breath caught in her chest.

"I'm asking if you will marry me," Paul said. Before she could answer, he rushed on, "I know what I said before, but I see now that you being a midwife is what God wants for you right now, and that doesn't take anything away from our marriage, if you'll say yes that is."

Blood pulsed through Elizabeth's veins triple time, and there was a rushing sound in her ears. She had been praying so hard for this very thing, and now that it was happening she knew that she needed to pray. *Lord, please show me what You have planned for me. Amen.*

As Paul reached over to take her other hand, he said, "And I know now that you should deliver babies as long as you can, as long as the Lord wills it. I will never stand in your way again."

That was the answer to her prayer. She opened her eyes wide as tears pooled in the corners, and she whispered, "Yes. I will marry you, Paul."

Paul leaned over to seal their engagement with a kiss, and Elizabeth felt God's peace descend upon her. She was glad that the two of them had gone through this rough patch because now she knew how to listen for God's will in her life. And that was the most valuable thing she could ever hope to learn.

9 798224 558292